DIANA
and the Journey to the Unknown

Also by Aisha Saeed

Diana and the Island of No Return

Diana and the Underworld Odyssey

★ ★ ★ WONDER WOMAN™ ADVENTURES ★ ★ ★ ★

DIANA

and the Journey to the Unknown

Aisha Saeed

Random House New York

Wonder Woman created by William Moulton Marston

Jacket art by Alessia Trunfio

Visit us on the Web! rhcbooks.com

Educators and librarians, for a variety of teaching tools, visit us at RHTeachersLibrarians.com

Library of Congress Cataloging-in-Publication Data is available upon request.
ISBN 978-0-593-17841-6 (trade) — ISBN 978-0-593-17842-3 (lib. bdg.) —
ISBN 978-0-593-17843-0 (ebook)

Printed in the United States of America
10 9 8 7 6 5 4 3 2 1
First Edition

For Nani

Chapter One

Where am I?

Diana spun in complete and total darkness. Had it been seconds since her journey began? Minutes? *Months?* Time had lost all meaning since she'd grabbed the metal bar fragments of an Underworld cell from her nightstand. The world around her had blurred into an endless expanse of inkiness. Gone were the walls of her room in the palace at Themyscira. Her bed. The soft white rug spread across her marble floor. Gone, too, was Cylinda, who'd scrambled from her guard post, racing to rescue Diana before she vanished. She had not succeeded.

Diana clenched the glimmering fragments from

the cell tightly in her hands as she hurtled deeper and deeper into the inky abyss. At midnight each night, these enchanted bars had transported caged children to parts unknown. Diana had lashed at the cage with the Lasso of Truth when she'd gone to the Underworld to rescue her friends. She'd managed to break a hole in the bars that was big enough for her friends, Imani and Sakina, to slip out of the enclosure and escape through Doom's Doorway to Themyscira.

Diana never imagined she'd voluntarily grab on to those same bars, which she'd carried home with her, to send herself straight into the clutches of evil—but no one knew *where* to find Zumius. And no one knew who or what he was. But with each passing day, they *did* know that the powers of the gods who ruled the world grew weaker and weaker because of him. Diana had decided to take the risk: to clutch the fragments when they began glimmering on her nightstand at midnight—and see for herself where they took her. It was an impulsive decision, she knew. But she hoped that maybe by holding on and transporting herself, she could find the kidnapped children. Maybe then Zumius could be taken down once and for all.

But as she hurtled onward, Diana's mind filled with doubt. Were the bars, in pieces as they were, malfunctioning? Might they leave her suspended in this darkness for eternity?

Suddenly a burst of warm air wrapped around her. Heaviness pressed in from all sides, squeezing her like a vise. Then Diana began to free-fall. Her heart somersaulted as she spiraled down, down, down. Curling into a ball, she braced for impact.

With a painful thump, she landed on hard concrete. She opened her eyes, wincing, and rose to her knees. She was in a cage in a windowless room. The walls were painted maroon, with golden trusses along the ceiling. *What is this place?* Diana wondered. How far was she from Themyscira? Were the other children here? Was Zumius?

Inching a hand forward, she brushed her fingers against the rounded bars. They were sandlike and grainy in texture, similar to the cage she'd broken her friends out of in the Underworld. Pressing her hand to her side, a touch of relief went through her:

the Lasso of Truth was still attached to her belt, as was her emerald-encrusted sword. She'd helped her friends get out of a cage exactly like this once before, Diana reminded herself. She'd help *herself* out now.

Diana gingerly stretched her arms and legs. Her head throbbed like a drum. Her entire body ached, but, to her relief, no bones seemed broken. Craning her neck, she peered out through the bars of the cage. Most of this tiny room was taken up by the enclosure itself. She could make out the edge of a skylight above, from which moonlight shone into the otherwise windowless room. Across from her was the only door, metal and locked with seven enormous bolts.

Diana strained her ears for the sound of footsteps or any sign of life outside the door, but all was eerily silent. For now. Soon enough, *someone* would arrive. Maybe Zumius. Diana shivered. She needed to act fast. She had to break out of this cage. Get out that door. Leave before anyone found her. The children who'd been kidnapped *had* to be trapped in other parts of this building. She'd heard that these children, unlike Diana herself, had special abilities. All she needed to do was reach them and help them get free. Using all their powers collectively, they could take down Zumius once and for all. There was no time to lose.

Diana gripped a bar of the cage with one hand. With the other, she reached for the lasso at her waist. She rose to her feet, ready to strike at the bar, but as her head grazed against the low ceiling of the enclosure, an alarm blared within the room. A whirring noise sounded from above. Diana winced and looked up—had she triggered this siren when her head touched the ceiling? The blare grew louder. But the whirring sound terrified her more. Dread filled her body. She'd heard that sound before: in her bedroom back on Themyscira, when the green-cloaked Targuni had tried to kidnap her. The creature had jutted out its arm and whirred with a noise much like this before launching a stream of golden powder into the air, obliterating a book into dust. The same powder had wreaked havoc on her people. It had toppled statues and pockmarked her homeland with craters. And now, with the same mechanical whirring buzzing above her head, she was trapped. Diana pressed herself against the back wall of the cage as a warm mist burst from above and sprayed down. She coughed. The room filled with the scent of mint and crushed cloves. Pinching her nose, she tried not to gag, but the smell was overwhelming. Mist dampened her hair and coated her cheeks and nose.

What is this? She wiped away the wetness with her hands.

Moments later, footsteps clicked in the distance. Then voices rose.

"Honestly, Serg! These things malfunction twenty times a day," a woman's voice said. "You act like it's an intergalactic emergency each and every time."

"I'm sorry, Dr. Reid, but we gotta check, just in case. His orders."

Diana tensed. Whoever it was, they were right outside the door. She watched as the first of the seven locks turned. It was too late for her to break out unnoticed. She glanced down at her sword; it was sheathed at her side, and her lasso was still in her hands. She couldn't let them find her weapons.

Not while she was still figuring out the best move. Without her sword and lasso, she'd have no chance against whatever or whoever was on the other side of the door.

Slowly the second lock clicked.

Then the third.

Diana slid her belt around until the sword was out of sight behind her back. After unfurling the lasso, she hastily wrapped it twice around her waist. She knotted it at the front into a bow, hoping it now resembled more a bulky belt than what it truly was.

The fourth lock turned.

Diana straightened nervously. Her head bumped against the ceiling again. The alarm blared louder. More mist rained down on her.

One by one, the rest of the locks unlatched.

Slowly, the door opened. She had no idea what was on the other side—and she was not looking forward to finding out.

Chapter Two

Two people entered the room.

The woman wore a white lab coat, and she had short brown hair. Dark glasses framed her eyes. She had yet to look up. Her attention was singularly focused on a thin, glowing rectangular device in her hand. The man who accompanied her appeared to be at least seven feet tall. He had a thick beard. His helmet and outfit were black, with a yellow feather emblazoned across his chest. A menacing brown nightstick rested at his side. He stared at Diana like he'd seen a ghost.

"Uh, Dr. Reid . . . ," the man said.

"Can we get on with it?" The woman tapped on

the tablet-like device. "Let's mark it and move on. Hand me the sign-off sheet."

"Um, I think you might want to take a look."

She pursed her lips and lifted her gaze. Her eyes met Diana's. Startled, the woman took a step back.

"Well. I see," she managed to say.

"Told you it wasn't a false alarm!" Her companion grinned triumphantly.

Stay calm, Diana told herself. *Play dumb until you can figure out what you're going to do.*

"Clearly, Serg," the woman muttered. "Let's get her situated if she's coherent enough to speak."

"I'm not sure the charm deployed," he said slowly. "She doesn't *seem* groggy at all."

Diana looked at the beads of cool liquid trailing down her arms. She certainly didn't *feel* groggy.

"Nonsense. She's practically a walking zombie," Dr. Reid responded curtly. "The records indicate the mist deployed not once but twice."

"I guess." The man eyed Diana uncertainly. "It's weird, though, isn't it? She came out of nowhere, and at *this* hour? We barely have a skeletal staff."

"You, scared? Serg, she's a third of your size," Dr. Reid said with a snort.

"I'm just saying. If she's one of *those* kids, her size doesn't matter. You've seen them," Serg replied defensively. "The metal bender nearly ripped the door apart when the charm wore off a smidge. And Aiko had my arms go soft like jelly without even touching me before we got the second dose on her."

Diana startled. *The other kids.* They'd been in this cage, too. So they *were* here!

"Be that as it may, she's under *twice* the usual dose, and she's definitely not one of those kids," Dr. Reid said. "There's a protocol to prepare for their arrival. Some sort of glitch must have occurred. It's not the first time."

"But what if she *is* one of them?" the guard insisted.

"Then I'm pretty sure we can handle her for a short while, until we send her off to the next location to join the other kids."

The *next* location? As fast as her hopes had risen,

they fell. If the kidnapped children weren't in whatever building this was, *where* were they?

"Let's get this going. I've got a mountain of work to get through," Dr. Reid said. She looked up from her tablet and directly at Diana. "What's your name? Identify yourself."

Despite her greatest efforts to seem neutral, Diana glared at her.

"I'll try again." The scientist's lips curled into a smirk. "Your name. What is it?"

Diana did her best to conceal her frustration and appear under the influence of whatever substance the mist had deployed. There was no way she was telling them anything.

"Probably useless to interrogate her now," the woman told Serg. "Because of the extra dose, we'll have to wait until it wears off a bit. Shouldn't take more than a few hours. Once she's come to, we'll figure out what happened."

A few hours! That was more than enough time, Diana hoped, for her to break out of here and figure out her next steps. If the kids weren't in this building, she'd find them wherever they were. She'd broken these bars once. She'd do it again.

Dr. Reid lifted her tablet and pointed it toward Diana. Diana flinched as a bright light flashed, followed by a clicking sound. "I'll send the photo on," she told the guard. "It'll take a moment for the feed to reach him, but he'll give us answers if she can't."

"Should I take her to the interrogation room?" Serg asked. "That way she won't keep accidentally triggering the mist?"

"Good idea." She nodded. "But put on the heavy-duty restraints. *If* she has powers, there's no telling what they might be."

The guard reached into his pocket and fished out a metal ring of keys.

An interrogation room? Restraints? Diana's heart sank. If he was going to tie her up, there would be no opportunity for her to break out, like she'd planned. She looked at the wide-open door. This would have to be it—her one chance to get away. This could be the best shot she'd have.

Can I fight both of them? Diana wondered. If it

came down to it, she supposed she could. But the best plan would be to take the duo by surprise and slip out the door before they realized what was happening. They thought she was sedated. She could use that to her advantage.

"And if she's not one of the kids?" Serg asked. "Then what?"

"Not our problem." Dr. Reid shrugged. "That's what the Targuni are for."

Diana shivered. *The Targuni.* Those creatures didn't run so much as fly. They had stopped at nothing to capture children on behalf of Zumlus. They were here, wherever *here* was. Of course they were.

The guard fumbled the keys in his thick fingers. "We've got to color-code these," he grumbled. "Too many to keep track of." At last he brightened. "There we go."

Dr. Reid lifted the tablet to her mouth and spoke into it.

"Subject is an adolescent girl," she said in a dispassionate voice. "Unresponsive to questioning. Will be transferred to interrogation room, with extra restraints employed as a precautionary method. Will resume questioning in two hours, once the charm's effects lessen. Press send."

Serg unlocked the cage. The door creaked as he began to slowly open it. Within seconds, he'd grab her and take her away. Fighting him could be tricky. And if she did get out, where would she go? *Stop,* Diana told herself. She'd worry about the next step when it was time to worry about it. Right now, she had to focus on the task at hand. Diana tried to steady her breathing. Right now, the door was opening.

"Signal is bad here," the scientist grumbled, tapping the rectangular device. "You got this?"

"Sure thing," the guard replied.

Dr. Reid hurried out of the room. Her shoes clicked against the floor, growing more distant with each step.

"And now for you." His hands rested on either side of the cage. "Let's go, come on over."

Diana pressed her back against the rear wall.

"Come on." His voice hardened. "I know you can walk. The charm doesn't render you immobile."

Diana kept her expression as blank as possible.

"You're frustrating, you know that?" He leaned in and reached out to grab her. His fingers were inches away. "I don't get paid enough for this gig," he grumbled to himself. He leaned into the cage. Moments later, he was *climbing* into the cage. On all fours, he made his way toward her and reached out to grab her by the ankle. Now was the time! Diana dove over his outstretched arm.

"What the—?" He startled. He swept a hand through the air to grab her leg but missed. Diana deftly landed on the floor outside the cage. She was out!

"Get back here!" He rose. "Hey! Ow!" The blaring alarm sounded again. A familiar whirring noise filled the room. Mist sprayed down, coating the inside of the cage. "You can't . . ." His voice faded. His eyes grew heavy, and he fell to the floor.

Diana broke into a run down the empty hallway. As she glanced around, she felt worry rise within her. *Now what?* She'd completed the first step and escaped from the cage—but she had to figure out her next move: getting out of here to reach the kids, wherever they were. Any moment now Dr. Reid or *someone* would discover the sedated man. They'd send guards and soldiers to hunt her down. She *couldn't* get captured again. If she did, she might never find the missing children.

CHAPTER THREE

Diana raced down the narrow hallway. Bright lights shone above as she swept past window-less room after windowless room. Glancing inside each one, she saw only empty cages. *Dr. Reid and Serg were right.* The other kids were definitely not here.

Sweat trickled down Diana's brow. The farther she ran, the more endless the hallway felt. At last, she skidded to a stop. An unlit corridor lay to her left. She had no idea where it led, but it felt safer to flee under cover of darkness. Turning, she headed down the corridor and raced as it snaked left and right and left again. *Where is the exit to this place?* Diana wondered frantically. At the end of the hallway, she reached a closed door. Pulling out her sword for protection, Diana gingerly turned the door handle. She stumbled into an empty room with sickly-yellow lights flickering above. Papers and pens were strewn messily across tables.

Windows! Diana brightened. One whole wall was lined with windows.

Diana grabbed a chair and pushed it toward the glass. Rising onto her toes, she strained until her fingers reached the top of a bronze-colored latch. *Will it open?* she wondered. Or would the windows be sealed shut, as they had been in Hades's home in the Underworld? Luckily, the glass windows parted without issue. Looking outside, Diana felt a touch of relief—she was on the first floor of the building; getting out would be easier than she'd thought. Cold wind swept into the room. Diana gripped the edge of the windowsill and, grunting, pulled herself up and hopped outside.

I've done it, Diana thought with relief. She'd made it out. She shivered as the icy wind whipped against her face. Flecks of white swirled around her. They kissed her face and her hair. The ground beneath her was white and powdery soft. It was *snow,* Diana realized.

Until now she'd only read about snow in her school lessons. Themyscira remained tropical year-round. As Diana looked at the white landscape, she wondered, *How far from home am I?*

A metal fence lined the perimeter of the building, which looked as though it had been dipped in steel. Diana tried to run toward the enclosure, but the snow was deep. It slowed her pace and left an unsettling trail behind her. Reaching the barrier at last, Diana craned her neck upward. The fence was metal with diamond-shaped spaces, easy enough to climb over. But she grew still. Above her was the moon. Or rather, *moons.* Three, to be exact. They shone brightly upon her. Panic bubbled within Diana. Wherever she was, she was *very* far from home.

Focus, Diana told herself. She pushed down her growing dread. There'd be time to panic later. There was only one thing to do in this moment: get out. The chain-link fence seemed two stories high. Something green sat atop its entire length. She'd need to climb this barricade and jump over to the other side. The missing kids were out there somewhere. Finding them was all that mattered.

Diana gripped the fence. It was wiry and rough against her fingers. She pressed her toes into the diamond-shaped mesh and started to climb. The fence swayed with her weight, but thankfully, it didn't give. As she made her way up, a familiar smell wafted toward her. Diana tilted her head, trying to place the sweet, unsettling scent. It was like honey, but not quite.

Roses.

Diana tensed, half expecting to find a Targuni crouched behind her, ready to drag her back to the building. But no one was there. Beyond the fence lay a wide expanse of snow and little else, save a sparse forest of some sort to the left of the building. At least, it *seemed* like a forest. The limbs of the trees were blue, and the moonlight revealed leaves of green, pink, and aqua. Hooking her feet and her fingers into the fence, Diana deftly continued her climb. Near the top, she scanned the surrounding area. She had no idea which direction to head in from here. There was no sign of any other building or structure as far as she could see. Moving toward the trees seemed to be the safest bet, she decided. At least it offered some hope of concealment from the guards who would inevitably be searching for her at any moment.

Just then she paused. Up close, she saw what the greenery lining the fence was: thorns. Enormous ones. The size of her fingers. Diana lightly grazed the tip of one and drew a sudden intake of breath—its cut was sharp and stung her finger. The thorns looked firmly attached, jutting from the top of the fence in both directions, ready to tear into anyone or anything that dared brush against it.

Diana debated her options. She could try to jump over the thorns, but if she didn't clear them, the resulting injury could affect her ability to escape. Maybe, she thought, she could tear off a section of thorns with her sword to safely get over to the other side? But was her flimsy sword up to the task?

There was only one way to find out.

With one hand, Diana continued to grip the

metal fence. With the other, she carefully reached behind her body and pulled out her sword. This was certainly no butterfly sword, which was designed to slice quickly and efficiently. But flimsy or not, this weapon *had* gotten her out of many a scrape in the past week. Diana pressed the sword flat, edging it under the blanket of thorns. Gently she scraped. The thorns clung stubbornly along the fence. Gritting her teeth, Diana shivered against the cold. She had minutes, maybe only seconds, before someone discovered she was missing. She needed to act forcefully. Squaring her jaw, Diana brought her sword down onto the greenery with all her strength.

Success! A thorn chipped off and landed on the powdered snow below. Heartened, Diana continued hacking at the bed of thorns. More and more greenery tumbled to the ground. At last, with enough space to safely cross, Diana tucked her sword away. Gripping the metal edge of the fence, she pulled herself to the top and swung her legs over the fence. The thick snow coating the ground blunted her fall. As soon as she landed on the other side, bright lights fastened to wooden poles around the fence flooded the area. A pulsing alarm began to blare at full volume, vibrating against her body. She took off in a run as a woman's voice sounded in the cool night air.

"Alert!" It was the scientist, Dr. Reid. "Code four. Dispatch the Xerx. Repeat: Dispatch the Xerx."

Xerx? Diana sprinted toward the strange forest. She had no idea what a Xerx was, but she knew she did not want to find out.

Chapter Four

Icy wind whipped against her face as Diana ran. Unlike the compact sandy beaches of Themyscira, the snow was thick and cold, rising to her knees and making her strain with each sunken step. She panted for breath. The forest's edge grew closer and closer. Once she reached the tree line, she could hide behind a trunk and figure out what to do next. Until then, she was exposed.

A faint buzzing began. Barely a whisper.

Diana hardly paid it any mind at first. But soon it grew louder. And angrier. Glancing back, she saw a sight she'd never seen before. In the distance, flowing across the horizon, were narrow-bodied flying creatures. They resembled dragonflies but were much larger, the size of crows. Their wings glowed bright against the darkness. There were dozens of them. Maybe hundreds. They were far enough away at the moment, but they were barreling straight toward her. Soon they'd be at her heels. Diana ran faster. The cold wind picked up speed, beating against her face as though conspiring to push her backward. Diana's face blistered from the frigid air, but she kept running. She had to get to the tree line, where she'd have a much better chance of hiding for cover. There wasn't a moment to lose.

Clenching her jaw, she pumped her arms and legs faster and raced with all her might. Her legs ached from the pressure of running through snow, but she didn't stop until, at last, she reached the first pale blue limb and, exhaling, pressed her back against the tree trunk. It was warmer within the trees. Heat seemed to pulse from the trunk. The dirt beneath her feet was inexplicably snowless and dry.

She peeked back toward the horizon. Her stomach fluttered. The creatures were still on her tail. Which made sense—she'd practically created a path for them to follow with her snowy footsteps.

She glanced about, but there were no bushes or hideaways to slip into to escape their notice. She peered at the trees. The limbs were high, but maybe she could lasso herself up and hide out among the leaves until the Xerx passed. It might not work, but it looked like the best chance she had. Quickly, she removed her lasso from her waist and knotted it. She snapped it toward the lowest branch. The rope encircled it. Diana tugged to hoist herself up, but the limb cracked. It crumpled to the ground. She ran a hand over the branch—its texture was like that of an eggshell. Diana tucked her lasso away. The tree was far too fragile to climb for safe harbor.

The buzzing grew louder. It shook the ground beneath her and ricocheted within her body. The Xerx were close. Within seconds they'd reach her. Then what? What exactly did they plan to do with her? She hurried through the forest, searching for somewhere, anywhere, to hide. Racing from tree to tree, at last she spotted a bright light in the distance. Diana made her way toward it, but as soon as she came close enough to discern what it was, her heart sank. It was a pond of sorts, set a few paces beyond the trees. It was petal pink and glowed in the darkness.

Diana shivered. Even if they hadn't spotted her yet, the Xerx knew she was there—the forest would be the first place they'd check. And with potentially hundreds of them searching, they'd find her. But jumping into this curiously colored water and holding her breath—they might not expect that. Her footprints would vanish. Any scent they might have been following would also disappear. Still, Diana gazed down at the water with hesitation. The thought of voluntarily diving into an arctic pond in the middle of a snow-surrounded forest felt as tempting as splashing into molten lava.

Just then, the dragonfly-like beings zipped into the forest. Leaves fluttered in their wake. Diana pinched her nose. She drew a deep intake of breath and slipped into the pond, careful to make not so much as a splash. Fully submerged, Diana braced for the cold, but to her surprise, the water was warm—pleasantly so. And without any effort, she sank to the bottom. *What sort of water is this?* she wondered. Was its warmth due to a thermal spring beneath the ground? That would explain the warm trunks and the snowless dirt beneath the trees just steps away from this body of water. Whatever the reason, she was grateful.

Diana looked up at the sky through the pink-tinged water; the moons gazed down upon her. Tensely, she waited. She prayed that her plan would work. Half a second later, a loud noise thrummed in the air above her—it vibrated the water, sending out ripples. Moments later the first of the Xerx flew overhead. There were so many that they blurred into one long, snaking line above. There were definitely hundreds of them, their wings translucent and flapping wildly. What would they do if they caught her? Diana shuddered. She did not want to find out.

Diana waited until the last of the stragglers had fluttered past. Her lungs felt like they were about to burst. Painfully, slowly, Diana counted to sixty, to be sure. She swam to the surface. Panting for breath, she surveyed her surroundings. It had worked! There were no Xerx in sight. At least for now.

As she stepped out of the pond, her clothing and her hair dripped water, which quickly froze into icicles. If she'd been cold before, she had no words for how chilly she felt now. Diana hugged her arms to her body and shivered. Teeth chattering, she looked around. Snow fell in thick sheets beyond the forest, and though it didn't stick to the warm dirt beneath her, soft flakes landed on her nose and face and blurred her vision. Hurrying through the forest, she tried a different direction. There had to be a place she could hide here, a burrow or a cave. But even with the leaves of the trees blunting some of the heavy snowfall within the forest, she could hardly see a thing.

Diana's heart hammered in her chest. The Xerx would circle back sooner or later. Whatever they were, they wouldn't stop until they'd accomplished their mission. And what *was* their mission, Diana wondered. To bring her back to the building or . . . to kill her? Tears stung Diana's eyes. She tried wiggling her toes; they were growing numb. Her fingers were also losing sensation. She could hardly feel her face.

Breathing heavily, she leaned against a tree. Her body trembled involuntarily, trying in vain to keep her warm. After everything she'd been through, was she really not going to be able to help the kidnapped children—the very thing she'd set out to do? Was she going to die of frostbite in a strange land far from home? Regret pooled thick and deep inside her.

Diana thought about her mother, Queen Hippolyta. Aunt Antiope. Cylinda and Yen. They were probably beside themselves with worry and anguish. She couldn't imagine the guilt Cylinda was feeling. She'd been charged with keeping an eye on Diana, and it was under *her* watch that Diana had vanished into thin air. Right this very minute, Diana knew, the women of Themyscira were terrified for her safety, wondering where she'd disappeared to. But glancing around, even *Diana* had no idea where she was. Looking at the snow-filled sky, she wondered how she could help the kidnapped kids if she couldn't even help herself.

Slowly, the snow began to ease up. Diana looked toward the land before her and squinted. Something was in the distance. A house. It had a rounded roof, and its chimney billowed lavender-colored smoke into the air. Warm light emanated from its windows. Ten feet behind it was an enormous mushroom-shaped structure. It stood taller than the home, with spotted red and white patches. She had no idea if whoever lived within the home would give her shelter or turn her over to the Xerx, but the mushroom structure seemed unoccupied. Maybe she could take cover there until she figured out her next steps.

Diana ran toward it, praying that the dark of night and the falling snow would cover her tracks. To her relief, as she raced closer, she saw no one near the structure. Stumbling under its roof, Diana exhaled. It felt warmer beneath it. She pressed a hand against the stem and was surprised to find that it felt spongy. So, it really *was* a mushroom! An enormous one. Aprons hung from copper hooks along its gills. On the ground, stacked against the stem, sat simple wooden crates. This appeared to be a storage area for the home.

Diana shivered and looked down at her soaking

clothes. The mushroom was a temporary refuge from the relentless snow, but it couldn't replace a heavy jacket and a scarf and winter boots. She squeezed her tunic, trying to expel the excess water. Her clothing crunched—the liquid that had soaked in was already solid ice.

Diana gazed at the house. The warm lights and spiraling smoke from the chimney beckoned her. She longed to knock on the door. Take her chances. But what if the home belonged to one of the guards? Or Dr. Reid?

Diana sniffed the air. The rose scent was back, the one she'd smelled when she climbed over the metal fence. It was stronger now. Diana grew cold. This fragrance had filled her entire bedroom when the Targuni had tried kidnapping her. Diana shifted her gaze toward the horizon. Just past the dwelling, the moons shone down upon roses. Rows and rows of them bloomed bright and beautiful, extending into the horizon despite the frigid temperature. Yellow, pink, blue, purple, brown, and even charcoal gray. Some were similar to the ones growing on the manicured bushes at home in Themyscira, but some were enormous, with thorns that looked to be practically the size of her palms; the petals were as large as Diana herself.

A chill of fear went through her. Now she understood where she was. This was the land of the green-cloaked creatures. The Targuni. The ones who had terrorized her and haunted her dreams. The ones who'd broken into Themyscira's impenetrable land and taken her best friend, Sakina. Who had blasted pockmarks onto her island and toppled the statues of the gods. The ones who had infiltrated a force field and kidnapped Imani. The ones who would stop at nothing unless *they* were stopped.

This was where the bars had taken her. Directly into their clutches.

Diana turned toward the forest she'd just come from. What now? Her knees felt like they were about to buckle. Where could she possibly find sanctuary in the land of the enemy itself?

Creak.

Diana jumped. Something shifted behind her. She jerked back, and her stomach turned.

There it was. Steps away. They were practically face to face. A cloaked being shrouded in green. In their hands was a sharp metal weapon practically the size of their own body.

A Targuni.

Chapter Five

For five tense seconds neither of them moved. Diana tried her best not to tremble. She knew the creatures were fast—so fast they practically flew. And she was on *their* land. How would she defeat the Targuni on their own terrain? There had to be hundreds of them. Thousands. Millions?

Focus, Diana. At the moment there was but one standing before her. And it *was* dark out; Diana knew the Targuni's vision was poor without sunlight. She couldn't outrun this being, she decided, but she could fight them. Diana carefully removed her lasso from her waist.

"I want to leave in peace. I want no trouble," she

said in a low voice. "Please leave me be, and I'll be on my way."

The creature tilted their head; their expression was unreadable beneath the cloak. The shears in their hands glinted menacingly in the moonlight. The Targuni hadn't moved. *Yet.* But she knew all too well that when these creatures did move, they moved with unrivaled speed.

"I'm warning you. Leave me be," Diana said. "I don't want to harm you, but I have taken down another like you. I *will* do it again."

The Targuni looked at the glinting metal in their hands, then back at Diana. *They're debating how to grab me.* Diana cringed. She had to do it. No part of her wanted to relive the moment in her bedroom, but she couldn't get caught. Not when the children were somewhere nearby. Not when she was probably so close to finding them. With trembling hands, she tied her lasso into a loop. Weariness passed over her. Her feet and hands felt like blocks of ice. She was too tired and weak to fight, but what other choice did she have? The lasso properly knotted now, she tried to reason with the creature one last time.

"This rope has felled your people before," she said. "I've watched them destruct into a pile of golden powder and debris. I don't want to do this. Please let me pass in peace."

The Targuni tilted their head. They moved toward her.

"You were warned," Diana muttered to herself. In an instant, she lashed her lasso at the creature. She didn't wish them harm, but she was *not* going to let them capture her.

The Targuni ducked. The tip of her lasso slammed against the mushroom, breaking off a chunk. Flinging the lasso again, she aimed at the creature, but the Targuni was fast—as fast as she knew their kind to be. The Targuni held their weapon up as though aiming for her. Diana gritted her teeth. *Not on your life.* She swung the lasso again as the Targuni flew to the side.

Without explanation, the creature stumbled backward. Turned around. They were leaving. Heading off to alert others, no doubt. Asking for backup. How many others would return to fight her? Diana clenched her jaw. With all her might, she flung the lasso toward the retreating figure. The rope landed with a loud *thwack* against the Targuni's side. The creature lurched forward, bending at the waist. Diana lashed out again. The Targuni stumbled to the ground.

This was it! With a swoop, she lassoed the creature with a final flourish. The Targuni rose unsteadily to their feet. They tugged at the rope encircling their shoulders, pulling frantically, struggling to break free. Diana tightened her grip. The Targuni were powerful, but they stood no chance against her Lasso of Truth. Diana drew the rope closer and closer. The last time she'd captured one and tried to remove their hood, the Targuni self-imploded violently, flinging Diana backward against a wall. But if the creature didn't destroy themself, they would destroy her. She inched the struggling Targuni toward her until they were practically nose to nose. Her entire body trembling, Diana reached a hand toward their cloak. She squeezed her eyes shut. Yanking the cloak off, she tensed. Waiting.

Nothing happened.

Diana opened her eyes.

The Targuni's cloak *had* fallen from their head and rested around their shoulders. But the Targuni hadn't imploded. Instead, Diana stood face to face with a fragile-looking creature. They had pale blue skin, with translucent yellow eyes and large ears that drooped to their shoulders.

Diana hadn't seen anything like this before, but one thing about the Targuni was unmistakable: their entire body quaked with fear.

Chapter Six

"Please don't hurt me," the Targuni croaked with a thin, rasping cry. They tried pressing their hands together in a plea, though the rope was so tight they could barely move. "I'll give you whatever you want. Gold? How about roses? I have plenty of both. They're yours for the taking."

What is going on? Diana stared at the Targuni. "I . . . I don't understand. *You're* the one who crept up on me," she said. "You're the one holding the metal weapon."

"My gardening shears?" The creature gasped and released the tool, which tumbled to the ground. "Oh, dear. I apologize if you felt threatened in any way. No. No. I only arrived at my work space to tend to my roses. My other supplies are in this shed. I came to fetch an apron." The Targuni gestured to the hooks hung with flowing aprons along the mushroom's gills.

Gardening shears. It was dark out—and Diana had been caught off guard. But now it was clear as day: the Targuni had held a pruner in their hands, for the roses in the distance. She looked back at the trembling being.

"My place is that way." They pointed to the warmly lit home. "Take whatever you wish. Just please don't hurt me."

"Don't hurt you?" she repeated. Her head throbbed. She thought of the relentless creature who had attacked her in her room. On the conjured lands of the gods. "But your people were the ones who hurt me."

"It's not possible," they whispered. "I've never seen you before in my life. Targs is my home, and I've never left it. Those are my roses beyond the fence. My most prized possessions. I was on my way to prune and water them when I chanced upon you. It was clear you were lost. I thought I'd see what the matter was. Forgive me. I only wanted to help."

Wanted to help. Diana felt sick. With the Lasso of Truth still wrapped tightly around the being, she knew that every word they said was true.

"Please. Please spare my life," they whispered.

Diana stared at the Targuni's tearful expression. With the hood around their shoulders, the creature stood half a foot shorter than herself. She glanced at the metal shears lying discarded at their feet. Horror swept through her as the reality of the situation landed on her with full force: In this moment, *she* was the one with a sword poised at the Targuni's midsection. *She* was the one who had wound a rope tight around their body.

Diana had been through so much in the past week. She had scaled a booby-trapped island of no return and sidestepped steel claws and metal arrows meant to maim her and her friends. She'd fought off hypnotized villagers and destroyed a demon dead-set on kidnapping them. She'd fought sea creatures in the deep blue ocean, traversed the Underworld, and battled undead monsters and Hades himself.

Danger seemed to lurk around every corner. She had proven to herself she was a capable and strong fighter. But she *only* fought in self-defense. It was the unspoken rule she lived by. She was never the aggressor. Not ever. But right now, as the Targuni trembled before her, pleading for mercy, her blood ran cold. *She* was the one who had threatened this being. *She* had entered their storage area. She had picked up her weapon to fight. She had been the aggressor. Right now, this was exactly who she was.

Diana removed the rope from the creature's body. Her hands trembled, but the chill running through her was not from the arctic temperatures.

"I'm—I'm so sorry," Diana said. "I was hunted by your people, the Targuni, earlier. They attacked my land, Themyscira. They kidnapped my friends. They tried to kidnap me. I'm on the run from them. When I saw you, I assumed you were here to capture me."

"If my people tried to harm you and your friends, that is unconscionable," they said. "But *me* try to kidnap you? If you judge me by the worst of us, would it be fair to judge you by the worst of your people?"

Diana thought of Hades. He was from her world, but would she ever want to be likened to him?

"You're absolutely right," Diana began. Before she could say more, a flash of pink and blue glinted beyond the horizon, and a faint buzzing floated in the air. The Xerx. They were heading back toward her once more.

"That noise." Diana pointed to the horizon shakily. "Those buzzing creatures are after me."

"The Xerx are out looking for *you*?" The Targuni's voice rose. "They are only sent out for serious matters."

"I am definitely a serious matter for them. I have to run. I have no idea what they'll do to me. But I am so sorry for what I did to you."

Diana glanced at the snowy horizon. She'd run to the tree line and head for the lake. She had to keep outmaneuvering the Xerx until she knew *where* the kids were located. Before she took off, the being gripped her elbow and spoke urgently.

"They'll find you. Grab hold of my shoulders. Now!"

The night sky was filling with glowing light. Her

pursuers were minutes away. But trusting a Targuni after all she'd been through? The buzzing grew louder. She had to decide. Time was running out. Diana swallowed and laced her hands around the Targuni's shoulders. The Targuni heaved her firmly upon their back. The scenery blurred around Diana as she was whisked toward the cabin. Her arms wrapped tightly around the green cloak, Diana shivered at the memory of a situation much like this not so long ago. Then she had fought against her cloaked assailant with all her might. Now she was relying on a Targuni to save her. Her mind understood that she needed to take this chance, but her heart still hammered frantically. After everything she'd gone through—was she really trusting a Targuni with her life?

Chapter Seven

After flinging the front door open, the Targuni rushed into the home and released her. Racing to the windows, they drew the curtains shut. Locked the doors. Diana bent at the waist, catching her breath. The home was as cozy inside as it had seemed from the outside. A fire burned in a fireplace across from her. Unlike the yellow and orange hues back home, the flames here were pink and lavender and smelled sweet, like honey. The warmth was welcome against her soaked skin.

The Targuni placed a finger on their lips, urging Diana to stay silent. A few moments passed before Diana heard the now-familiar buzzing outside the home. Diana didn't move a muscle. The noise grew louder and louder. The Xerx were above the house at this very moment. The floor vibrated beneath her feet. Would they sense her presence? she wondered. Thirty excruciating seconds passed before the noise at last receded. But for the crackling of the fireplace, the cabin was silent once more.

Only now did Diana allow herself to relax the slightest bit. As she edged closer to the fire, her clothing and hair dried almost instantly, but when she flexed her hands and toes, she swallowed: they were completely numb, and her fingers were blue. She could barely move them back and forth.

"Looks like you've a bit of frostbite there. Don't fret," the Targuni said. "Happens when you're not from here. Go on and sit closer to the fire." They nodded to brightly colored toadstool seats set around the fireplace. "I'll bring you a tea that should clear it right up."

Diana sat down on a yellow toadstool. It was sturdier than it had seemed. Glancing around, she noticed the cabin was small and simple, made from the trunks of the colorful trees of the forest she'd traversed through. A table and a pair of chairs were tucked into a corner. Paintings of roses adorned the walls. A staircase led to a second floor.

The Targuni opened the cabinet of a wooden armoire and pulled out a container of leaves, a cup, and a saucer. They tossed the leaves into a pot hanging over the flames and, moments later, poured out a steaming drink.

"There we go. Drink this." The Targuni handed Diana the saucer and cup. "Warms you from the inside out. Cures frostbite or numbness in a matter of seconds."

Diana savored the warmth of the cup in her hands. Gingerly, she took a sip. The liquid tasted sweet, like a flower. As she drank it, her bruises and aches began to vanish.

"Thank you," she said. She looked down at her hands and her feet, sensation now returning, the discoloration fading. "My toes and fingers were completely numb. I could barely feel my face. There's nothing like this back where I'm from. You saved my life."

"Frostbite is a common enough ailment here. I'm happy to be of help."

"I'm . . . I'm Diana."

"My name's Inya. Now, be sure to drink it to the last drop. There's more where it came from should you need it, but you'll be good as new in a few moments."

Diana fixed her eyes on the steam rising from her cup. She was still trying to process what had happened. A few moments earlier, Inya had been tied up in her lasso. Diana was grateful no harm had come of the incident, but guilt still pulsed through her veins. Diana knew she had every reason to be afraid of the Targuni after everything she'd been through. Her reflexes were tense. *Of course* she was on guard. But that didn't change the fact that if she had succeeded and Inya had self-destroyed, it would have been an enormous tragedy and injustice. One for which Diana would have been entirely responsible. Diana looked at Inya and tightened her grip on the cup. Despite what Diana had done, Inya had shown her kindness in return. Diana vowed then and there she would never make a mistake like that again.

"Tell me," Inya said. "What brings you here to our lands?"

Diana glanced around. "I'm not even sure where *here* is."

"Targs is the name."

"The name of this city?"

"Planet. Not a big one, mind you. You can traverse the whole of it on foot in ten days or so, but it's big enough for everything we need."

"Do you have any idea how far I might be from home? From Earth?"

"Earth? Can't say. But we're at least ten light-years from the closest planet with known life. Safe to say you are quite a ways from this Earth planet you call home."

Ten light-years. Diana's head spun with this new information. She thought of the bars she'd gripped and the darkness that had followed. It'd felt like an interminable amount of time, but light-years? She never could have imagined they'd have transported her quite this far.

"But we must do business with your people if I can understand your language as clearly as I do." Inya peered at Diana curiously. "Did you get mixed up in a portal on your way to somewhere else? Happens sometimes. I'm sure we can sort it out and get you where you need to be. We don't get visitors too often—must be why those Xerx were chasing you.

"I remember the last time someone accidentally wound up here." Inya sipped some tea. "Poor thing walked around for days, completely terrified. Thought he'd lost his mind."

"Your portals," Diana said, thinking of the cages. "Were they glimmering ones? Made of a sandlike substance?"

"They do glimmer. But only when they're set to transport." Inya nodded. "We use them to travel and sell our wares across the world. There's quite a demand for our work. Our rose petals have medicinal benefits, and the thorns are always in demand, used for protective gear of all sorts."

"That must be how I got here," Diana said. "I was transported while holding on to bar fragments. They shimmered at midnight and deposited me into a cage here in Targs."

"A cage?" Inya lowered the cup. "Did someone

reconfigure portals into *cages*? Can that even be done?"

"Seems so," Diana replied. She relayed to Inya some of what she'd been through and how she'd chanced upon the fragments of the bars to transport herself.

"Cages." Inya grimaced. "Portals are made in that building, but it sounds like they've been repurposed to more sinister ends. Why would someone do such a thing?"

"I overheard that the kidnapped children I'm searching for are kept in another location," Diana said. "Do you have any idea where it might be?"

"Can't be on this land." Inya shook their head. "The portal center is the only building like it here, and the work done there is outsourced to people from worlds beyond ours. Other than that building, there's little more than markets, farmlands, and workshops for our welders and makers."

"So the missing kids aren't here, on Targs?" Diana's stomach sank.

"I highly doubt it."

A banging noise sounded at the door. Both of them leapt to their feet.

“Open up!” a voice shouted on the other side. “Now!”

Diana looked at the trembling door. Whoever was on the other side was there for her.

Chapter Eight

The pounding against the front door continued so roughly that a photo fell from the wall and crashed to the floor.

"Open at once!" a masculine voice thundered.

Diana's heart thudded. If the person got in and saw her there, cup and saucer in hand, Inya would face consequences for harboring her.

"Go upstairs," Inya said. "Just past the landing is a room with a chest set to the side. Can't miss it. It should be more than big enough to hide you. It seals good and proper. You wait there while I get him to go away."

The pounding grew louder.

"Go on," Inya said urgently, waving a hand. "Before he breaks this door down."

The door shook, practically coming off its hinges. Whoever was on the other side would surely stop at nothing, least of all a locked chest, to find her. And in the process he'd turn this entire home upside down. She couldn't risk any harm coming to Inya. She knew what she had to do.

"I'm going to leave," Diana said. "So long as the rear of the house is unguarded, I'll go out the back window and let him catch me. This way he won't know you helped me."

"What? Listen to me. There's no safe harbor out there," Inya told her urgently. "The farmhouses are scattered throughout the lands, and I cannot say if others will take you in as I have. Not for certain, anyway."

"I have to get to the kidnapped children," Diana said. "It looks like my only way to get to them is to let the kidnappers find me. Maybe they'll take me to where the children are being kept."

"And what if they try to kill you instead?"

"They won't." Diana's voice wavered. But Inya could be right. They could simply consider her more trouble than she was worth. But what was the alternative? She had to try.

Diana retied her lasso and fashioned it back into a belt. She tucked her sword behind her, praying no one noticed her weapons. Girls were so often underestimated. This time, she was counting on it.

A loud *thud* sounded as something slammed the door. A crack split through the center of the wood.

"You have ten seconds or I knock this entire door down!" the voice shouted.

"Thanks again for all your help," Diana whispered.

"Ten!"

"Wait!" Inya ran to the stove and picked up a tin box. Returning to Diana, the Targuni placed eight gold coins in her palms.

"Nine!" came the voice again.

"Are these . . . are these made of gold?" Diana looked down at them.

"They should help you in your journey."

"This must be worth a fortune. I . . . I can't take this."

"Gold has true value," Inya said. "In a pinch, it can come in handy, for its language is universal. Keep it in case you need it."

"Eight!"

"Thank you," Diana said. She glanced at the window. She needed to leave before the door broke down.

"Seven! And I'm beginning to grow angry," the voice on the other side bellowed.

Diana pushed open a back window. The path was clear. Her feet sank once again into the frigid snow. Her heart pounding as the gold coins jangled in her pockets, Diana raced around the perimeter of the home to the other side. A large man, similar in size to the guard she'd subdued, stood by the entrance.

"Two!" he shouted. From his profile, she saw his expression was flushed.

"Looking for me?" she asked loudly. "Over here!"

The man swiveled. Meeting her gaze, his eyes narrowed. He lifted a whistle and pressed it to his lips. The piercing sound echoed into the sky. Diana flinched, covering her ears. A faint sound emerged. It grew louder and louder. The ground beneath her trembled. There they were—the Xerx. They swept toward her. Diana hunched her shoulders. Doubt filled her as they zoomed full speed at her. What if Inya was right? What if—

In a millisecond, the swarm was at her heels. Lunging, they lifted her up. Diana fell backward, and then, as though she were riding on a flying palanquin, they sprinted into the night sky. Twenty Xerx zipped to either side and encircled her wrists to restrain her. With alarming speed, they darted higher and higher. Diana shivered as they swept over the peculiar forest, the thermal pond, and the open fields of snow until at last the building dipped in steel with barbed fencing appeared in the distance. *This is the only way,* Diana reminded herself. But as the building grew closer, uncertainty pulsed through Diana all the same.

She had to rescue the children. She had to end Zumius's reign of terror.

But one question remained unanswered: *Could she?*

Chapter Nine

The creatures dove through an open metal door, Diana in tow. They zipped down the very hallways Diana had raced through a few hours earlier. Abruptly the Xerx swooped into a room. They tossed her into a metal cage, where Diana crashed to the floor. The door clicked shut. Scrambling, she pressed her back against the bars. This room also had windowless maroon walls, but it was three times as large as the previous one. There were other cages in here, too. Save her own, all were empty.

"Restraints," a woman's voice coolly said.

Dr. Reid stood in the corner of the room, tablet in her hands, her lips pressed into a thin, straight line as she looked at Diana.

A guard approached. Reaching through the gates, he grabbed Diana's arms, tying them to the bars. Within moments she was bound.

Five guards stood by the front door. They held menacing nightsticks.

The scientist approached Diana. "You had some nerve, trying to escape," she said tightly. "Though I suppose we can thank you for exposing our safety lapses. Now, let's get started, shall we? You can begin by telling us who harbored you just now."

Diana glared at her and said nothing.

"I'm not in the mood for you to play coy." Dr. Reid's voice rose. "The Xerx searched for you everywhere. You were nowhere to be found. Your hands and legs appear fine. Clearly, after as long as you were out there in the subzero tundra, that's scientifically impossible. Someone aided you. Someone gave you medicine."

Diana wanted to laugh at this woman's question. Did she honestly think Diana was going to tell her anything?

"Staying quiet isn't an option, I'm afraid." Dr. Reid

drew closer. "We can do it the easy way, but I'm amenable to doing it the hard way as well."

"I think it was Inya," the guard who'd captured her said. "Found her near the cabin."

"Inya," the scientist repeated. "That should be an easy enough question to solve. Let's bring Inya in and get to the bottom of it."

No!

"No one helped me," Diana said hurriedly. "And I turned myself in, didn't I?"

"Ah, so she does speak," the scientist said. "Serg, can you come here, please?"

The guard whom Diana had trapped in the cage earlier entered the room. His eyes were red and watery.

"I'm in no mood to drag matters out," the scientist told Serg. "Time is of the essence, especially with the alignment fast approaching. We need to figure out where in the universe this loose cannon came from and what to do with her. I'd say a few demonstrations of exactly what you're capable of might have her willing to answer more questions, don't you think? Mind having a one-on-one with this girl?"

"I'd love to." His smile revealed two newly missing teeth. "As a matter of fact, there's nothing I'd like more."

"I don't think Zumius would like it if you harmed me," Diana said. There was no sense in playing coy. She needed to get to the other kids. The sooner the better.

"Zumius?" the scientist repeated. Her eyes narrowed. "How do you know his name?"

"When someone's hunting you, it's pretty hard to forget."

"Who are you?" the woman spat out.

"Diana," she responded simply. "My name is Diana, princess of the Amazons."

"Diana." The woman straightened. "Th-there's no way. He would have informed us before such a transfer."

"She's lying. Probably saw the name on one of the files when she was running around through the building," Serg said. "She *did* break out of an office window."

"*That* makes more sense." The scientist's eyes narrowed. But before she could say anything else, a voice cried out from beyond the room.

"Stop! Wait!" Hurried footsteps sounded outside. Diana watched the metal door push open forcefully. A reed-thin man with hair sticking straight up raced past the guards and to Dr. Reid.

"Don't . . . do . . . anything . . . ," he panted, bending at the waist.

"What is it?" The scientist stamped a foot impatiently. "We are in the middle of something important here."

"Zumius," he said between breaths, and quickly shut the door. "The picture you sent. He responded. I-it's her." He pointed to Diana. "It's the girl he's been waiting for. Diana."

Silence filled the room. The guards' jaws dropped. Everyone stared at Diana as though she were a ghost.

"You're Diana?" the toothless guard said.

The room burst with noise. Guards and scientists chattered over one another.

"I don't understand. This little thing is the girl

he's been going on and on about for the past year?" Dr. Reid thundered.

"Must be *something* to her," another guard murmured. "She *did* escape, when no one else has."

"Why did she arrive at midnight?" Dr. Reid fumed. "We put in the protocols, and he just sends in people willy-nilly whenever he wants to?"

"She wasn't on the roster. He didn't know she had arrived," the man panted. "I think she came on her own."

"On her own? Ah." Dr. Reid gazed at her, realization spreading across her face. "Did you think the other children were here? Came to save the day, didn't you?"

Diana felt her cheeks grow warm.

"Zumius," the man said. "H-he wants her brought to him at once. Warned she's tricky, though, so be careful."

"Tricky." Dr. Reid snorted. "What an understatement. Go get the maximum dosage. I don't want to make a mistake this time."

"But the maximum is enough to put down an elephant," the man said.

"He said she can't escape under any circumstances, right?" She glared at him. "Well, that'll do it, won't it? It'll definitely put her to sleep." Turning to one of the guards, she ordered, "Go get the pipe. We'll hose her down."

Moments later an enormous pipe appeared. Three guards grunted as they lifted it, their expressions strained. The pipe's golden rim was now aimed directly at her.

"On the count of three," Dr. Reid said. She moved to the back wall and crossed her arms.

"One," a guard began.

Diana pursed her lips.

"Two."

She shut her eyes.

"Three."

A burst of liquid slammed Diana square in the jaw. The force of it shoved her backward. She coughed as warm liquid dripped down her throat and coated her body. A metallic scent filled her nose. She tensed, waiting for the charm to put her to sleep. Seconds passed. Then minutes. Diana thought of the eternal sleep that Augustus had misted through her palace home in Themyscira at the start of the Charà festival; it had knocked everyone out, but it had no effect on her.

The cloud of mist subsided. All eyes fell on Diana. She leaned back, pretending to go limp. The sooner they got going, the better.

"Finally," Dr. Reid said triumphantly.

The man punched some buttons on the wall. The door to the room creaked open. A guard cut off Diana's restraints and hefted her over his shoulder. Cautiously, the scientist moved closer to her. She pressed a cool finger against Diana's throat. Diana tried her best not to flinch.

"She's alive," the woman said dryly. "Just as the boss ordered. Now get her out of my lab before she does anything else. I've had enough adventure for a while."

Diana was carried down the hallway. Her head bumped against the guard's rough armor. She hated that they thought they'd won. But the children were not here. Zumius was not here. She needed to go where they would be.

At last they arrived in a different room. She was

lowered to the floor of a new enclosure. They roped her hands to the gritty glimmering bars.

"Good riddance." Serg folded his arms. "Can't say I hope to see you anytime soon."

The feeling's absolutely mutual, Diana almost retorted. But within seconds, the cage shimmered and shook. Diana felt her body trembling and shivering before everything around her blurred.

The world went dark once more.

Chapter Ten

Diana's breath caught in her throat. She'd been swept into this same spiral not long ago, and the weightless, inky nothingness sent fear down her spine.

How long has it been? Diana wondered as she spun, barreling through the darkness. And *where* was she going this time? There were no guideposts or gradations of dark to chart her journey—no method to determine whether she was heading closer to home or farther than she'd been before. Dizziness filled her senses. She curled herself into a ball and tucked her chin against her knees. There was no telling when she'd arrive—it was best to brace for whatever impact was to come.

Suddenly gravity pressed against her once again. She was falling. Faster and faster until—*thwack.* With a painful thud, Diana landed, knees first, against solid ground.

She cried out in pain. This landing was rougher than the last one. Her knees screamed in agony, scraped and bleeding. Her head throbbed. Opening her eyes, she squinted at the sudden brightness of the room. It was daylight here, wherever *here* was. Sunlight poured into the room from small rectangular windows framed at even spaces along the top of the walls. A songbird peered in through one of the windows, its gaze landing on her.

Diana winced as her eyes adjusted to the light. She took in her new surroundings. Unlike the cold steel building she'd come from, this entrapment was inside a home of some sort. Cream sofas faced a brick fireplace with lit candles inside it. A long rectangular mirror framed in gold rested atop the mantel. A silk rug, pink and detailed with octagonal patterns, was spread on the floor. In the distance, an open door revealed a perfectly made bed with pastel sheets. Two bored-looking guards in black-and-yellow uniforms sat on stools, their backs against the walls. They guarded the carpeted stairs across from her. They seemed half-asleep; they hadn't acknowledged Diana's arrival at all.

As Diana stood, her legs felt shaky. She checked the ceiling, hoping not to trigger any sort of misting charm, but the roof of this cage was higher, and nothing but smooth metal looked down at her from above. She glanced around. Were the other kids somewhere in this home, too?

"You okay?" One of the guards rubbed his eyes and glanced her way. "Landings can be rough."

"She's fine, Eliot." The other guard yawned.

"I dunno. She's bleeding a bit. Couple of scrapes, it seems." The guard named Eliot leaned back and squinted. "We'll get you a bandage next time one of us heads out."

"Ah, just a surface wound," the other scoffed. "She'll get over it."

Diana pressed her hands against the cage. Where did Zumius find people like this? People willing to sell their souls? Who didn't bat an eye while aiding someone intent on destroying the world?

Tentatively, Diana traced the bars of the cage. They were sandlike and grainy. The same ones she'd broken her friends out of. It would be a lot more complicated to break out of a cage under the supervision of two guards. But at least she had a chance. As she looked around, the biggest question remained unanswered: Where was she?

"Guess we should let the boss know she's here, whaddaya think?" one of them said.

"Suppose so." Eliot leaned toward the floor and picked up a gray rectangular device. Lifting it, he twisted a knob. It crackled to life, static sounding from it.

"The subject has arrived," he said into it. "Approximately two minutes prior. Is conscious and speaking."

Another scientist. Diana tried her best not to show her frustration. More interrogations and prodding. The room trembled. A gust of wind blew through Diana's hair. Then, from nowhere, appeared a person—if one could call him that. He was nearly ten feet tall, and the top of his head grazed the ceiling. He wore a black bodysuit with yellow feathers printed all over it—but unlike the guards, his entire body seemed to glow and shimmer as though alight with a thousand diamonds. His face was masked. Diana stared at him. The outfit looked so strange—almost comical—and if he weren't so terrifyingly tall, towering over her, she would have laughed at how silly it all looked.

But nothing about this *felt* silly. This was not another scientist, Diana realized with a shiver. This was him. Zumius. The one who had haunted her days and her dreams. Who tormented the gods and stole their powers. The one who wanted to destroy all she loved and held dear. He'd torn apart so much, hurt so many, and now he stood right in front of her.

Diana clamped her fingers around the bars so tightly, her knuckles turned white. She thought she'd feel afraid if she ever met him, and though her nerves felt raw and exposed, the biggest emotion coursing through her was not fear. It was fury. The way he looked at her with triumph—trapped as she was—burned.

"Now, I must say, it's cute watching you try not

to get mad." He took a step toward her. His voice was nasal-sounding, with a high-pitched lilt. "Imagine this," he continued. "I comb the world—or more accurately, *worlds*—looking for you. I set an ungodly—pardon the pun—bounty on your head. It piqued *quite* a bit of interest, I'll have you know. But somehow you got away at every turn. And now *poof!* You magically show up like a hand-delivered gift all wrapped up in a bow. I can't predict you, can I, Diana? But riddle me this: How did you make your way to a portal without getting caught?"

"Where are they?" Diana asked in a low voice. Her fury was so hot she could taste it on her tongue.

"You mean the others? Don't you worry. You'll meet them in no time."

"How could you?" she asked. "Stealing *children*?"

"You make it sound like they're toddlers learning to walk," he said with a laugh. "None of you are ordinary children, now, are you? And if I'm to benefit from such powers, don't I better my odds by grabbing abilities from scrawny kids rather than fully grown superheroes?" He tapped his head. "Now, *that's* smart thinking, I'd say."

"You won't get away with this," Diana said. "Mark my words. The gods—"

"The gods!" He clapped his hands and howled. "They're frazzled as can be, aren't they? Hades was dishing out the yummiest gossip before they neutralized him. But the fact of the matter is it's too late for any of your gods to actually do anything at this point. I'm almost done. I've got you now, and after I get the other kid—which should be any minute—it'll be over tonight, as soon as the moons line up for five full minutes a quarter after midnight. It won't happen again for another month, so your timing was perfect. I really couldn't have scheduled it better myself."

"If you think any of us would work for you," Diana said, "you're completely mistaken."

"Oh, you will." His lips curled. "There's no question about that. You might be powerful, but you are hopelessly naive. Ahh—" His eyes shone. "Did you come here to save the kids? You did, didn't you? Well, let's hear it for unearned confidence! Wanting to save everyone, like you had any kind of chance.

Now, enough chitchat." He moved closer. "I'm dying to know: What exactly is your superpower?"

My superpower? She stared at him.

"Now, don't play coy with me." He lowered himself until he was eye to eye with her. "I've heard lots of things. Your flying ability, for one. But there must be more than that. You don't get a reputation as the most powerful kid in the world without a bit more up your sleeve."

Flying? If the circumstances weren't so dire, Diana could have laughed.

"Seems like the intelligence you received about me was rotten," she replied. "I have no powers. And I definitely can't fly. Sorry to disappoint."

"I believe my sources were correct." His voice grew hard.

Diana felt sick. Not only was Zumius evil, but he was relying on hearsay and rumors. He had caused so much harm in his pursuit of her, all based on misinformation.

"Oh, come on. I deserve to know what I'm dealing with." Zumius drew nearer. Diana's breath caught.

He was so close. So close she could reach through the bars and touch him. Diana inched her hand behind her. Her fingers grazed the hilt of her sword. After what almost happened with Inya, even attacking someone clearly evil like Zumius made her feel a little nauseous. But she'd have to handle him in order to have any hope of helping the missing children.

"Well, if you are demanding, I guess I have no choice but to tell you," she said quietly.

"Speak up," he shouted.

"I can't just blurt out my most dangerous skills, can I?" she continued in a low voice.

Zumius drew closer to her. His face was directly in front of the cage. Inches away. Her body shook. She knew she'd only have one opportunity. She'd need to make it count—there was no room for error. In a flash, she yanked her sword out and struck it straight through a space in the bars, intending to pierce Zumius in his midsection. But instead of making contact, the sword flew straight through him, landing on the floor behind him. Diana's breathing grew shallow. The demon she'd encountered on the land of Sáz was also not solid in shape; her hand had burned from the touch of his formless, gaseous body. But right now there was nothing to touch at all. Not only had her sword gone through him—her whole arm had. It was as though he weren't even there. Diana yanked her arm back and clutched it to her chest in surprise.

"Nice try, attacking a hologram," he said with a laugh, staying exactly where he was.

Eliot stood from his stool and walked over to Diana's sword. With a kick from his steel-toed boot, he spun the weapon forward, and it slipped beneath a white sofa, out of sight.

A *hologram*? Her mind raced. Did Zumius mean to say this wasn't actually a real person standing before her? Was this a three-dimensional representation of Zumius? But if he wasn't here, then *where* was he? She hadn't come this far to have him *continue* to evade her! Diana's eyes blurred with tears. Zumius was not here. She was still trapped. And now her sword was gone.

"Was that really the best you could do?" He seemed disappointed. "How you managed to get away from me this long is super confusing now. Doesn't matter what sort of flimsy weapons you have, my dear; it's over for you."

Diana looked at the sofa. A glint of green shone beneath it. She'd poked fun at her weapon earlier in the week, telling her mother it couldn't hurt a fly as she longingly eyed the butterfly sword, with its sleek metal edge and light handling. But her own sword had more than proven its worth. She'd used it to handily fight off enemies, both living and dead, supernatural guards and sea monsters more than twice her size. This sword had helped her out of the most trying of times. And now it was beneath a sofa, out of her reach. It was gone.

"How can you kidnap me without even knowing why you wanted me in the first place?" Her lips trembled. "I don't have the abilities you think I do."

"Don't want to share? Fine. Don't." He shrugged. "Once you're hooked up to the Splectra, all will be revealed in its own time."

"You won't win." She gritted her teeth.

"Funny words coming from the girl locked inside a cage." He cocked his head. "I believe I already have.

Aristaeus helps me control the winds. You wouldn't believe how handy it can be. Aiko's mind-bending is how I managed to snag the gods' powers in the first place. It's been a real trip to think their powers away. Lumierna's an easy favorite, too, though. Bending metal is just plain old *fun.* Though you, I have heard, will surpass them all."

"Sir!" Someone hurried down the steps and burst into the room. It was a woman. She wore the same uniform as the rest, but her left eye was red and swollen, and a welt was growing above her forehead. She limped forward. "I wanted to update you on the situation."

"Only one update I want to hear," Zumius said. His smug voice was replaced with one of clear annoyance. "Did you get her?"

"Unfortunately, I did not," she said. "But it wasn't for lack of trying. We did our best. Really, we did. The situation is tricky with the god squad stationed around the home, as they are."

The god squad? Diana's eyebrows shot up. Was she referencing the group of men and women who were tasked with performing missions for the gods?

"So what you're saying is you failed. Again." Zumius said angrily. Diana shivered. She knew what stood before her wasn't real. But nevertheless, the tension in the room rose exponentially. Even the bored-looking guards were attentive now. "If the Targuni could do it, I don't see why you and the others cannot do it, too."

"My sincerest apologies," she said shakily. "But, your greatness, the god squad, even though they're not at their full powers, were sent here by, well, *gods.* They've been standing watch night and day. They follow her to and from anywhere she or her mother might go. Yesterday, I managed to snag a uniform from a mail carrier to get there undetected, but the foursome got me immediately."

"That's just silly now. They can hardly walk around without stumbling lately. Their increased clumsiness corresponds with the gods' loss of their powers."

"Yes, sir. But they still can fight. They are *still* more powerful than us mortals."

"Quit with the excuses!" he snapped. "This has to be dealt with by tonight. Call in double the men.

Leonard"—he turned to the other guard—"walkie the backup. That way one set can distract them. The other can grab her. And you"—he jabbed a finger toward the woman—"head down the chimney. You're small enough, I think. And Imani's got the least impressive powers of any of the other kids—so long as she doesn't see you coming, you've got her."

Imani. They were going after Imani? Diana's body froze.

But . . . didn't Imani live in Atlanta?

And wasn't Atlanta in . . . the mortal world?

Diana's eyes widened. No. This couldn't be right. She'd misheard. She'd had to have.

"I'm . . . I'm not so sure about the chimney," the woman said.

Chimney. Diana thought back to her conversation with Imani—the Targuni had climbed down her home's chimney to try to grab her before. . . .

"You better *get* sure," he scoffed. "And don't forget to swing by the storage facility to get the truck and the extra crew."

"That's two hours away, sir," the woman said nervously. "Longer if there's traffic."

"So long as they're hooked up by midnight, all's well. And once you've got the backup crew *and* the truck, the god squad doesn't stand a chance. But any missteps," he said evenly, "and I promise you will not like what happens."

Diana's head throbbed. If she was close to Imani, it meant . . . *Diana was in the mortal world.*

Her breathing quickened. *Calm down,* Diana urged herself. She couldn't panic now. But it felt impossible to steady herself. Themyscira was a land created by her mother to be a safe space from the very place she now found herself.

"Leave Imani alone," Diana shouted. "She can't even help you. She doesn't have powers anymore. She's of no use to you!"

"I *knew* you were lying earlier!" Zumius declared triumphantly. "Imani has no special skills, either, eh? Her powers have been documented by my own men. Nice try, though."

"She *had* powers! Past tense. Zeus took them from her. I was there when it happened. She can't help you. Leave her alone."

"Her powers were taken, you say?" He paused,

considering this. "Ah, set to dormant, you mean. Why, this is the best news since your capture! She won't be able to blend her way out of this. Once we get past the stumbling, fumbling god squad, she'll be easy enough to pluck away."

"What? No." Diana's breathing grew shallow. How could this have made Zumius happier? How did she make things worse?

"Should I bring her here, sir?" the woman asked. "Or take her straight to the Exodus tower?"

"Straight to the building," Zumius said. "Penthouse is all set up in preparation for their arrival anyhow."

"And her?" Leonard jabbed a thumb toward Diana.

"She'll stay here until the last minute. She's a slippery one, though I do have an ace up my sleeve that'll make her comply when the time comes."

The gray speaking device buzzed against Leonard's hip.

"Code two," a male voice said amid a crackling noise.

"Ah. Must attend to this," Zumius said. "And, Diana, my dear, we shall meet tonight. Until then . . ."

His image flickered before—*poof!*—vanishing.

The Exodus tower. Diana repeated the name over and over so she could commit it to memory. She had to get there before Zumius did. And more pressing, she had to get to Imani before his people did. But Diana looked at her sword, stuck under the sofa. How was she going to get out of a locked cage to free those children with two guards a stone's throw away? How was she going to navigate the unfamiliar terrain outside *in the mortal world,* find Imani's home, *and* find the Exodus tower?

She squeezed the bars of the cage and held back her tears. The burden of all she could not do rested like boulders against her shoulders.

Chapter Eleven

Diana paced the narrow space. *Focus,* she told herself. The first thing she needed to do was find Imani and get her someplace safe, which meant she needed to break out of this cage as soon as possible.

"I'm grabbing a bite to eat," Leonard said. He looked at Eliot. "Want anything?"

"Nah." Eliot shook his head. He glanced at Diana. "What about you? Hungry? Thirsty?"

Diana glared at him.

"Telling you. You're too friendly with these kids." Leonard shrugged. "Don't ask me later, Diana. I won't be giving you a drop."

"Don't forget the bandages!" Eliot said.

"How can you help him?" Diana said in a low voice. "You see it, don't you? He's evil. He's pure evil."

"Money's good." Leonard's eyes narrowed. "I'd say that's enough of a reason."

"Zumius, he's rough around the edges," Eliot interjected quickly. "And sure, this isn't the ideal way to go about it, but when he takes over, everything will change for the better. It'll all be worth it in the end."

"You can't really believe there's any way to justify kidnapping children," Diana said. "Nothing can be worth that."

"Ha! Like you're ordinary children," Leonard scoffed. "Truth be told, it's better you're all locked up. Don't want your kind roaming around unaccounted for. No telling what you'd do. Best to leave such powers in the hands of someone like Zumius, who can utilize them for what needs to be done."

Without another word he hurried up the stairs. His heavy footsteps vibrated above. A distant door opened and shut. Diana grazed her fingers against the cage. *Breathe,* she reminded herself. She couldn't get caught up in her emotions. She had to escape. Now. She looked at the bars. She could technically break out with her lasso. She'd done it before. But glancing at Eliot, she wondered what *he* might do when he saw her trying. He'd kicked away her sword. She couldn't afford to have her lasso confiscated as well. But there was only one guard at the moment instead of two. And the lower part of the cage *was* obscured from his viewpoint by the white sofa. If she had any chance of getting out of here, this might be it.

Untying the lasso from her waist, Diana secured it in her hand and, with all her strength, lashed at the bars. The cage shivered. The bars wobbled. Eliot glanced at her from his stool.

"Look, kid, I know you're stressed," he said. "But taking it out on the cage isn't going to do anything. Lumierna tried breaking out, too. They bend metal. If they were defeated by it, pretty sure you don't stand a chance of beating the bars into submission."

Diana ignored him. She couldn't fly like Zumius

thought she could, or metal-bend like Lumierna, but this *lasso* had true power. And it had helped her out in many situations, including getting a cage like this to break open enough for two girls to narrowly slip out. Now she prayed that it would do the same for her and that the sofa would obscure her work from his view.

Eliot stared at her, bemused, as she continued her assault. "All right." He shrugged. "Knock yourself out. Don't say I didn't tell you it was pointless."

So long as Eliot chose not to take her seriously, she had a chance to get out before he finally *did.* Diana struck the bars with the lasso repeatedly, with everything she had. Her arms grew tired; the bruises along her elbow ached. Was this cage trickier than the other one? Diana wondered. Or was she too exhausted? Diana didn't let up. Through the weariness, she kept going. Lashing out, over and over. The same spot. On the twentieth strike, a burst of powder broke loose. At last! She worked faster. Finally, a tiny crack rippled along the bottom four bars. She smacked it again. The opening widened. A chunk of bar broke off. As she lashed again, more and more crumpled to the floor. A small space broke open close to the ground. Maybe it was large enough to squeeze through.

"Look, you've got to calm down," Eliot said, glancing at her worriedly from his stool. "Want some ice cream? What do you say? Kids love ice cream."

This was it. Now or never. Diana dropped to the floor. She pushed herself out. The edges of the bars scraped against her, but at last her feet touched the carpet. She'd done it! She was out.

"Hey!" Eliot's eyebrows shot up. He hopped off his stool.

"Don't move," Diana warned. She gripped the lasso tightly. "I want to get my sword, and I want to leave. That's all."

"L-look, you can't just leave." He raised his brown nightstick with one hand and with the other grazed another weapon at his belt—something dark and metal. "Let's get you back in the cage." He looked over at the broken bar fragments. "I can cover the mess up easily. Super glue is amazing. Leonard doesn't even need to know it happened."

"I'm not going back in there. I'm leaving."

"Diana," he said with a sigh. "I don't want to hurt you. Go back in. Please?"

"Where is Imani?"

"Imani? Now what do you need to know that for?"

Diana didn't have time to negotiate. Leonard could be back any second, and it would be much harder to fight two. Swinging her lasso, she hurled it toward him. It launched into the air and wrapped itself around him.

"Hey!" He pushed against the rope. "Wh-what are you doing?"

The Lasso of Truth began to glow and shimmer.

"Get me out of here," he panted. He pressed his arms against the lasso as though he could burst it with sheer force. His cheeks turned bright red. A few seconds later, as she expected, his shoulders drooped in defeat. His head hung low.

"What do you want?" he asked softly.

"Where's Imani?"

"No." Eliot squeezed his eyes shut. "We can't . . . tell . . . you . . . that."

His face grew redder and redder. Diana smiled

a little. There was never any use trying to fight the lasso. It always drew out the truth.

"She's at the corner of Myrtle and Jasmine," he finally burst out.

"Where?" she said. "I need directions."

"You go down the block and head past the underpass. Then a few blocks left past the park. She's in Golden Bluffs. In a cul-de-sac. It's one of only a few developed properties after the strip of stores. Can't miss the white fence and the yellow chimney."

Block. Underpass. Golden Bluffs. The words passed over her like oil on water.

"Let's try this again," she said. "Give me directions like left and right, east and west."

"Okay," he whimpered. Tearfully, he gave her directions. Diana repeated them to herself, trying to memorize them.

"You've been a big help," Diana said.

"Are you going to kill me now?" Tears leaked out the sides of his eyes.

Kill you? She frowned. A part of her wanted to make him afraid. Even if only for a little while. He'd done so much harm to so many people. But she thought of Inya. She had vowed on Targs that she never would forget who she was. She was someone who helped those who needed her—and she would defend herself if necessary. But she would never be the aggressor. Eliot was subdued. He was no longer a threat. And she'd gotten what she needed.

In the silence, Eliot's lower lip quivered. "I was just following orders!" he sobbed.

"Following orders is not a good enough excuse for what you agreed to do," Diana said. "You're as complicit as Zumius. But I'm not going to kill you. I *am* going to make sure you stay out of my way, though. Where's the key for this cage?"

"It's right here." He nodded to his pants. Tears dripped down his cheeks. "It's in my pocket."

Diana yanked out the key and tugged the lasso, sliding the man across the floor toward the cage. It was not an easy task. Eliot was huge and brawny. Gritting her teeth, she moved him to the edge. After unlocking the cage door, she opened it.

"Get in," she said. "I need you out of my way, and this is the surest bet. Get in and I won't hurt you."

The man shuddered, but he stood up and climbed into the cage. In one fell swoop, Diana unfurled the lasso from his body and slammed the door shut, locking it with the key with a final twist. Tucking her lasso against her hip, she paused. A door creaked open somewhere in the house.

Diana hurried to the sofa, grabbed her sword from beneath it, and breathed a sigh of relief as she slung the weapon into her holster, exactly where it needed to be.

"Thank you." Eliot pressed his face against the bars. "You could have gotten your revenge. Thank you for not hurting me."

"You're lucky that's not how I work," she replied. "But while you're stuck in the cage, maybe take a moment to reevaluate your life choices? This can't be what you're willing to stake your life and soul on."

Footsteps sounded above. A door closed. Diana glanced at the staircase as the floorboards creaked. Leonard. He was back.

"Don't say a word," she warned Eliot. "You've seen what I can do."

Eliot paled and slowly nodded. Diana glanced at

the stairs in the distance. Leonard would be down here in a matter of seconds. She hurried to the side of the staircase. The element of surprise was her biggest strength.

"Got ya a cheeseburger," Leonard's voice called out. The stairs shook with his heavy steps. "They were out of American cheese. I went with pepper jack. And before you ask, *no,* I didn't get bandages—not until she asks herself. And politely!"

Diana held her sword securely in her hands. She wondered if Eliot would shout out and reveal her location. He worked for Zumius, after all, and while the Lasso of Truth could reveal what was true, it could not change someone's heart. Footsteps thudded. One. Two. Three. Moments later, she saw a steel-toed boot. This was her moment. Diana leapt in front of him. The guard looked at her, puzzled, and then—his eyebrows shot up.

"Eliot!" he began. "What the—"

But before he could finish his sentence, Diana struck her sword out, upending the food in his hands and splattering the cheeseburger against his face. Then she shoved him as hard as she could. He fell backward onto the carpeted floor with a loud groan.

Diana sprinted upstairs to the main landing. This level of the home was enormous, with wooden floors and three crystal-laden chandeliers. Expensive-looking rugs were spread out everywhere. Gentle music played throughout the space. Scanning the room, she finally saw it: a door.

She raced toward it and locked her elbows, ready to push as hard as she could against it. Surely it would be fortified. But to her surprise, the lock turned effortlessly. She pushed open the door. Blinking, she stepped onto a brick landing. The harsh sunlight made her squint. Large trees loomed around the front of the spacious house. She pressed the hilt of her sword nervously. The mortal world. She was here. Thousands of miles from home. And alone. But before she let herself go further down the web of worry, she paused. It would take Leonard a minute to realize that Eliot was stuck and to get him out, but she needed to *keep* the guards inside the house as long as possible. Frantically, Diana searched beneath the trees. At last she found a branch. Thick as her arm. She pressed it through the door handles. Hopefully this bought her some time. And she needed every bit she could get.

Chapter Twelve

Following Eliot's directions, Diana took off in a sprint down the street. As she glanced back, she noticed, to her relief, no one was chasing her. Yet.

A bright hot sun beamed down upon her. Compared to the cool wintery frost of Targs, Atlanta was a furnace. The farther she ran, the more beads of perspiration formed along her forehead. This place was busy. Despite the urgency of her situation, she couldn't help but glance at the commotion around her. Motorized vehicles sped down a road running parallel to her. People inside them scowled and sent loud honking noises into the air. There were shops up and down the walkway. People drank beverages at outdoor tables overlooking the road. But why? She scrunched her nose. To look at the vehicles? Practically everyone here had a glowing device in their hands, she realized the farther she walked, and every person she came across was glued to it as though the fate of the world rested within it.

Turn right. Diana skidded to a stop at the end of the block. That's what Eliot had said. Now she turned left at the third street. Then the next right, after that. At least, she *thought* it was the next right. *Breathe,* Diana reminded herself. Left was still left, even here. And east was still east. Relying on her memory, Diana kept walking. The roads grew less busy the farther she went. A woman walked by her with a dog restrained by a cordlike device. The woman had white wires coming out of her ears. Diana thought of Binti, who ran free wherever she pleased, and felt a pang of sympathy for this animal.

"Look, Mommy!" A child tugged on Diana's tunic. Glancing down, Diana saw a little boy holding his mother's hand and peering up at her.

"She's a superhero!" He pointed to Diana's colorful tunic.

"Um. Yes, honey. It's a great costume." The woman gripped the child's hand tighter and pulled him away from Diana.

Superhero? Zumius had used this word as well. What was *that*? Self-conscious, Diana looked around. With her blue and red tunic and boots, she *was* dressed completely differently from anyone here. She grew aware of the stolen glances in her direction by those she passed. Diana picked up her pace. The sooner she reached Imani, the better.

Turning a corner, she saw an expanse of meadow to her right. There were children everywhere, swinging and sliding on play structures. A trio were kicking a ball in the distance. Parents sat on benches, chatting. Some gazed down at the omnipresent rectangular devices. The grassy field was different than her own in Themyscira, but familiar enough for a pang of homesickness to twist within her.

From the corner of her eye, Diana saw a child who couldn't have been older than three. She was climbing the stairs atop a play structure with a narrow green chute spiraling down from the top. The child reached the platform, but instead of taking the slide, she tottered toward a set of evenly spaced metal bars ahead of her. They were ten feet above the ground. Diana smiled a little—the bars did look fun to swing from.

"Mama! Look!" the child cried out happily. She stood atop the first metal bar and raised her arms up with delight.

"Fiona!" Her mother leapt up. "No!"

The girl clapped gleefully before her expression shifted. Her body wavered. She was about to fall, Diana realized with horror. She was going to crash to the ground.

In an instant, Diana broke into a run toward her. She sped across the street, pumping her arms as fast as she could. The girl teetered, her arms flew in the air, and she slipped. She was falling. In a split second, Diana swooped the young child into her arms right before she hit the ground. The girl safely in her grip, Diana felt weak with relief. The little one looked up at her, her large brown eyes filled with wonder.

"Wow," she whispered in a hushed voice.

"Fiona!" her mother cried out, hurrying toward them. Diana let the girl go. Fiona hurried to her mother.

"Oh, thank goodness, you're okay." Her mother squeezed the child close. Diana smiled. She, too, had sent her mother into fits of worry many times herself.

"Th-thank you." The woman looked up at Diana. "She could've broken an arm."

"I'm glad she's all right," Diana said.

"But how did you do that?" she asked, hesitating. "You were on the other side of the road, weren't you? How could you get here so quickly?"

"Oh," Diana startled. She'd been noticed from afar? "I've always been able to run pretty fast."

"That wasn't fast," another woman said, approaching them. "It was miraculous."

Only now did Diana realize that the cheerful noises of children playing had completely vanished.

Everyone in the area, from the children to the adults, looked at her wide-eyed. A woman off to the side held up a rectangular device pointed straight at her.

"Cool outfit," said a girl, who gazed at Diana's tunic. "Did you make it yourself?"

"Are you magical?" a child with rounded glasses asked.

"No . . ." Diana's voice trailed off. She rose from the ground. "I'm just fast. Really." She backed away. "I, um, I have to go. Glad you're okay, Fiona."

"Bye!" the girl cheerfully called out.

Diana raced away before anyone could ask another question. She thought about their stunned faces and tried pushing her own confusion away. This was the mortal world. It was different from her own. Perhaps what was ordinary back on Themyscira, like running quickly, was seen as extraordinary here. That's all.

She turned down the next block, following the rest of Eliot's directions, until at last she saw a collection of homes behind a landscaped entrance. Golden Bluffs. Imani's home was there. Diana hurried toward it, but then her pace slowed. She thought of how everyone had looked at her at the park. It wasn't only how fast she'd run, but her clothing, too. A boy had tugged at her tunic earlier and called her a superhero. Whatever that meant, it was clear she looked like she didn't belong here. And she couldn't risk standing out—not when she was so close to Imani's home. Not when there were likely guards awaiting her arrival—surely Eliot had alerted them as soon as he could. She'd be spotted in a matter of seconds.

Diana gazed at a set of stores around the corner from the entrance of Imani's neighborhood. There were narrow spaces between each one. Hurrying down one of the darkened alleyways, she breathed a sigh of relief once she reached the back of the stores. The shops butted up to forested woods. As she hurried through the brown-limbed trees, a pair of deer and a doe scurried past her, but thankfully there were no people in sight. At last she saw it: a white picket fence and the back of a home with a yellow chimney. Flowers trailed the upper trellises. She could see oak and myrtle trees in the backyard. A tire swing hung from one of them. Imani's home.

She could run over in a matter of seconds. The fence seemed easy enough to hop over.

But then what?

What exactly did she plan to do? Break into Imani's home? Zeus had erased the girl's memories. Imani didn't even remember the full truth of who *she* was. If Diana burst in, Imani would rightfully see her as a stranger worthy of suspicion. But how could she explain it all in a way that would make any sense to someone who'd forgotten everything? She remembered how suspicious Imani had been last time, on the conjured land of the gods. She'd thought the Liara dragon was a lizard with glued-on wings! Would Imani ever believe her if she tried to explain?

Suddenly she jerked her head up. Two people—a man and a woman—emerged from the woods farther ahead. They had on black boots, and both wore awkwardly fitting pants and loose shirts. The man carried a blanket. The woman had a woven basket resting on her arm. Leaning down, the man spread the blanket on the grass behind Imani's home. As she smoothed it out, his eyes widened and he lost his balance and stumbled to the ground. Settling finally, they set sandwiches on their laps and looked intently at Imani's home. They weren't wearing the trademark black-and-yellow uniform of other guards she'd seen, whose attire was so unusual they could be spotted from a distance. Instead, these two sported ordinary pants and shirts she'd seen on many in the mortal world, and appeared to be having a picnic. Except neither of them touched their food. Their gazes were sharp. They sat with their backs fixed and straight. Were they the people whom the guard earlier had called the god squad? The ones sent by Zeus to protect Imani? Diana dug a toe into the dirt. How was she going to get around *them*? They weren't her enemy, but if they saw her, they *would* try to stop her. She could try to reason with them and explain the situation, but the chances of them letting her do what she needed to do were nil. She was Princess Diana of the Amazons. *A child,* as everyone back home always reminded her. In different circumstances, Diana would have asked them to join her to help, but she could see by the way the man had stumbled to the ground while simply laying out a blanket, the way they looked nervously about, that their powers weren't what they once were. Unlike Diana, who was wanted very much alive, Zumius would not think twice about harming them. She couldn't let that happen. Enough people had already been hurt.

Diana debated her options. She could double back and try her luck by entering the neighborhood from the other side, but there'd be other such guards protecting the front of Imani's home, too. And . . . glancing down at her tunic and her shoes, she knew that with her clothing and the lasso and sword at her side, she definitely didn't fit in here. They'd recognize her instantly.

Frustration tore at Diana. It wasn't like she needed to break out of a magically sealed home in the Underworld, or cross a river of burning lava, or destroy a dangerous demon here in the mortal world. But right now traversing the woods to get to Imani without catching the eyes of the god squad felt just as impossible.

Diana looked again at the pair sitting on the blanket. The woman tucked a strand of hair behind her ear and smoothed out her shirt. The coordination of their clothes was sloppy, yes. But their clothing *was* of the mortal world. *I need to camouflage,* she realized. She couldn't blend into things like Imani, but maybe she could dress up like a mortal and slip by everyone undetected all the same. Maybe then, she stood a chance.

Chapter Thirteen

Diana hurried back through the piney forest until she made her way down the alley and onto the main road once more. She looked at the storefronts she'd hurried past a short while ago. Scanning each one, she finally brightened: Chloe's Clothing. Heading toward it, Diana wondered how quickly they could prepare an outfit for her. Her tailor back home was fast, but even she took a full day to finish up a rush job. She stepped inside as the door jingled. Cool air blew against her face. The floor was a sleek, speckled white. Clothes hung on steel racks positioned throughout the tiny store. *How clever,* thought Diana with relief. Premade clothes would go much faster than she'd anticipated, so long as she could find ones to fit her.

"Welcome to Chloe's, please enjoy your browse." A woman with a blond ponytail sat on a stool, gazing down at a rectangular device resting on a clear counter in front of her.

"Thank you," Diana said. "May I try some of these on? They're lovely, but I do want to make certain they fit."

The woman jerked her head up. She took in Diana's clothing. Her eyes widened. Her mouth parted slightly.

"There are dressing rooms along the back wall," she said, clearing her throat. She pointed to a room in the corner with a curtain draped over it.

Diana pulled out a few pairs of jeans, a long-sleeved cream shirt, a few pairs of shoes, sunglasses, and a scarf. From a table with purses and handbags, she chose a brown leather one with flowers and two straps; she could easily store her original clothing inside it and wear it on her back.

Changing in the dressing room, Diana examined

her outfit in the mirror. With the glasses and the scarf wrapped around her head, she felt relieved. Her face was sufficiently covered. The pants felt a bit itchy and brushed roughly against the scrapes along her knees, and the long-sleeved shirt tingled against her arms, but the outfit change had worked. She could hardly recognize *herself.* The god squad would definitely not recognize her. She carefully tucked her sword beneath the back of the shirt to obscure it from view and belted her lasso.

"Thank you," Diana said when she exited the dressing room. "This should do perfectly."

"Are you sure about the scarf?" the woman asked. "It's kind of hot, don't you think?"

"It suits my needs perfectly," Diana said. "Thank you for all your help." She hurried to the door.

"Hey! Wait!" the woman called out. She stood up from her stool and placed her hands on her hips. She gazed at Diana in absolute bewilderment. "Aren't you forgetting something?"

"I am?" Diana said.

"Yeah," she said slowly. "You need to pay for the clothes."

"Oh. Right." In her urgency to get back to Imani before the guards arrived, Diana hadn't considered this. Of course this woman wanted payment. Except Diana didn't have any money.

"Can I come back a bit later and pay you?" Diana said. "I'm sure I can get my hands on whatever is required to pay for this soon enough."

The woman looked at her incredulously. "Listen. I'm sorry, but you can't walk out of here wearing merchandise without paying for it. I can put the items on hold for you. We do it all the time. Then you can come back when you have the payment, and it will be waiting for you."

There was no time! Diana's mind raced as she considered her options. She could easily run out of this store and be out of sight before the woman could do anything, but she didn't want to *steal* clothes!

The gold, Diana remembered. Inya had given her gold coins. She'd said it was a universal currency. And when else did she need currency as much as she needed it now?

"I don't have the money used by your people. But

maybe I have something that could work instead?" She rummaged through the bag.

"'Your people'?" the woman repeated. She frowned. But her expression shifted when Diana pulled out the coins and placed them on the table.

The woman picked one up. She squeezed it between her fingers. She stared at Diana.

Diana froze. Did people in the mortal world know about gold? Would she accept it as payment?

"Is this gold?" the woman asked incredulously.

"Yes!" Diana nodded with relief. "Would this be enough to cover my clothing?"

The woman stared at the coins. "I'm sorry," she finally said. "We take credit cards. Cash. Checks. But gold coins? No one's ever given me gold before as payment. And these are *heavy.* They must be worth a fortune. There's no way the clothing you're buying could come close to the amount these are worth."

"But nothing says you *can't* accept gold, does it? Please. It's all I have," Diana pleaded. "I desperately need these clothes. So much is at stake. So much depends on it."

The woman blinked.

"I swear on my soul the gold is genuine," Diana said. "Whatever is beyond the cost of the clothing, keep it as a gesture of my gratitude."

Diana's stomach fluttered as the woman debated what to do.

"To think I almost called in sick," she finally said. "Okay. Yeah. Sure. Gold for payment it is." She pushed the other coins back toward Diana. "I think one should more than cover this."

Thanking her, Diana raced out of the store and toward Imani's neighborhood. The clothing felt strange, and the saleswoman had been right—the scarf *did* make her feel warmer beneath the beating sun, but she looked at the people she ran past, and this time, though some appeared peeved when she cut in front of them to hurry faster, none of them ogled her like she was from a different planet.

Heart pounding, she walked past the crepe myrtles flanking Imani's neighborhood sign, Golden Bluffs. Homes in different stages of completion lined the street on either end. Workers with yellow helmets and vests hammered and drilled nearby. None of them glanced her way. She worked over her cover story as she hurried toward Imani's home. She was a friend of Imani's. Getting together for a hangout. There was nothing strange about her walking straight up to the front door and knocking on it. Nothing at all.

The neighborhood ended in a circular drive with three homes around it. Only the center home looked occupied. It had blue shutters and a yellow chimney. Imani's home. Two members of what could only be the god squad stood off to the side. One leaned against a light pole, reading a newspaper with the sleeves folded over his arms three times. The other wore ill-fitting pants and pretended to inspect the half-finished home next to Imani's.

Diana tried her best to appear cool and unconcerned. *Confidence,* Diana reminded herself. More than this costume she wore, she had to *act* like a girl from the mortal world if she was to be believed. Imani's door lay just ahead. *Walk up the steps. Ring the bell,* she told herself. *Convince Imani to let you in.* The last part, Diana knew, would prove trickiest. All the disguises in the world meant nothing if Imani refused to let her in.

A small vehicle drove past her. It pulled into Imani's driveway. Were Zumius's men in there? Moments later, instead of guards, a woman in a flowery print dress emerged from one of the doors. From the other appeared Imani. Diana startled. There Imani was. And she was okay. For now. The two of them walked into the house. Diana wondered if they took notice of the men next door in the vacant house pretending to examine the windows, but they showed no signs of paying them any heed. But as Diana looked back at Imani's house, a new reality hit her—not only would she have to convince Imani about what was going on, but she'd also need to convince Imani's mother. As Diana debated what to say, Imani's mother emerged from the house in a blue smock and matching slacks. She headed back to the vehicle. The engine burst to life, and then she backed out of the driveway and drove away.

Imani was home alone. This was her chance. Diana picked up her pace and headed up the walkway straight to Imani's door. She felt the curious gazes of the god squad upon her. But she was just a mortal girl out to visit a friend. So long as Diana pretended this was exactly what she was up to, no one would suspect a thing. Heart thrumming, she knocked on Imani's door.

Footsteps sounded on the other side. Diana held her breath. The door opened. There was Imani. At last, they were face to face. Diana felt as though she could scarcely breathe.

"Mom, did you forget something?" She paused and looked at Diana. "Hi. Uh, look, if you're selling something . . ."

Before she could finish her sentence, Diana spoke.

"Please," she said quickly. "I know you don't know me. I'll explain everything to you—but you *have* to let me in. It's a life-or-death matter. Please."

Diana tensed. Imani had to believe her. She had to let her in. There was no plan B.

Chapter Fourteen

For ten long seconds, Imani did not speak.

Diana fidgeted. Would Imani slam the door in her face? If the god squad grew suspicious, they'd wander closer. What if, despite her disguise, they realized it was her?

"Okaaaay," she finally said. She stepped to the side. Breathing a sigh of relief, Diana slipped into the carpeted foyer. The walls inside Imani's home were gray. Framed art from when Imani was younger hung on the walls alongside photos of her and her mother over the years. There was a cozy-looking family room with a teal sofa; a yellow fireplace sat across from it. Toward the back wall was a kitchen with a sliding glass door that led to a yard filled with flowers: geraniums, tulips, lilies, and daisies, and a simple bird feeder resting against a white fence.

"So, what's going on?" Imani crossed her arms. "You're in trouble?"

"Thanks for letting me in," Diana said. "I'm Diana. I'm here because our lives are in danger. Yours and mine. There are people looking for us. I heard with my own ears that guards are coming this way any minute to take you, so we need to get you to a safe place."

Imani stared at her.

"Cool," she finally said. "Now I think it's time for you to leave."

"I know how this sounds," Diana pleaded. "But it's true. There *are* people outside to protect you, but the incoming guards? They're bringing reinforcements. There's no guarantee the god squad can fight them off in the mortal world. The safest thing to do is leave."

"Evil guards? God squad? Mortal world?" Imani repeated. "Listen, my mom is *finally* letting me stay home alone tonight instead of carting me off to my aunt's. I never should have let you in, but you *really* have to go. Now."

"Imani," Diana pleaded. "I'm not explaining this properly. If you can hear me out—"

"How did you know my name?" Imani tensed. Her expression grew warier. "I've never met you before in my life. You're not in any of my classes." She looked at Diana's oversized scarf and sunglasses. "I'm pretty sure I would remember you."

"I don't go to your school. We met under different circumstances," Diana said.

"Yeah? When?"

"Um . . ." Diana hesitated, knowing how the truth would sound. "A few days ago."

"A few days ago?" Imani walked over to a glowing rectangular device, similar to the ones she'd seen people all over Atlanta gazing into. "I'm telling my aunt to come over."

"Wait. I'm not lying to you," Diana said in a rush. "I swear it. You don't remember because your memory was erased. I *know* how unbelievable this must sound to you, and I can explain it all in more detail later. But, Imani, your life is in danger. We should get you out of here and somewhere safe. I only want to help you."

Imani's gaze traveled to the hilt of Diana's sword glinting beneath her shirt.

"Who am I in danger *from* exactly?" Imani's eyes narrowed.

"The sword? It's for our protection." Diana gestured to the weapon. "You have to believe me, Imani. Please let me explain."

"You have five minutes," Imani told her. "Then I call my aunt."

"I'll be quick," Diana said. "But you have to know . . . the things I'm about to share with you didn't happen in the mortal—the human—*this* world where you live. I know how it will sound, but everything is true. Please keep an open mind."

"You have four minutes," Imani said tightly.

Diana launched into their shared past. She told her about the Targuni who had broken into her home in an attempt to abduct her. The palace of the gods on a conjured land created by Zeus. Their walk through an alpine forest to take in an ocean ribboned with red and blue. And the Targuni who had swept in and taken Imani.

"You were saving me when they took you," Diana said. "I was almost gone when you jumped out from where you'd camouflaged against a tree. You tried to keep me from getting kidnapped, and in doing so you were taken."

Quickly, Diana told her about Hades and the Underworld and the cage she'd broken the girls out of. The escape they'd made through a winding tunnel until they'd fought their way back to Diana's home of Themyscira.

"Zeus—your father," Diana continued, "he said you could stay in our world and learn more about your powers and who you were. He said returning to this world—the mortal world—with your memories and powers intact compromised your ability to live a normal life. You chose to forget. That is why none of what I'm telling you rings a bell. But it's all true. Every last word. And at this very moment, people are coming to your home to kidnap you. We *have* to get you out of here as soon as possible."

There was a long silence. Diana bit her lip. Would Imani believe her?

"Your time is up," Imani finally said. "I think you should leave now."

Diana felt deflated. Tears filled her eyes. Now what?

Imani's expression softened a bit. "Look, it sounds like *you* believe it. I don't think you're *lying* per se. But none of this makes any logical sense. You get it, right? Zeus is my father? He's a mythological Greek god. And powers?" she repeated. "I'm sorry, but none of this is actually possible, and I can't try to make you feel better and say I buy any of it."

"Well, how is it physically possible to contact your aunt using that rectangular thing?" Diana pointed. "Why is what I said any crazier?"

"You mean my phone?"

"Imani, please— Ow." She grimaced and grabbed her knee. With the pants chafing against it, the scrape from when she'd fallen into the cage stung more and more.

"Are you injured?" Imani asked.

"I'm fine," Diana said. "It's only a scrape."

"Looks like you're bleeding through your pants," Imani said, concerned.

Looking down, Diana saw a patch of red seeping through.

"That could get infected," Imani said. "Come over to the kitchen. My mom's a nurse; we have a million bandages and disinfecting wipes."

The kitchen was brightly lit with a wooden table off to the side and a counter with fresh fruit in a bowl. Imani opened a cabinet above a steel sink.

"Clean it up with this," Imani instructed her, handing her a white moist wipe. "It's an alcohol swab. Stick the bandage on after, it'll curb the bleeding."

"Thanks," Diana said. She rolled up her pants and wiped and taped up her injury. Though Imani didn't believe Diana, she was still kind to her, helping her. It broke Diana's heart to realize all their shared memories belonged to Diana alone.

"Just because you don't remember something," Diana tried again, "doesn't mean it didn't happen. You probably don't remember being a baby and crawling, do you?"

"Nice try. I'm not a baby anymore." Imani rolled her eyes. "And I do remember what I was up to a few days ago."

"I know things," Diana said. "Things only you could have told me. It proves we've met before."

"Oh yeah? Like what?" Imani said, slightly amused.

"Well, for example, the chimney over in the main room? The green-cloaked Targuni came down through it to kidnap you. You said you were getting ready to play video games in your loft and eat a bowl of cereal. *That* was actually the first time your mom let you stay home by yourself."

"My loft," Imani repeated. "How do you know my games are up there? Wait a minute. Have you been following me or something?"

"No!" Diana thought quickly. She had to give her more. Irrefutable proof she couldn't reason away. "When the green-cloaked creature came to take you, you ran out the sliding doors." She gestured to the door next to her. "You hid behind the bird feeder over there and—"

"So you peeked through my fence, too?" Imani interrupted angrily.

"You made the bird feeder in first grade," Diana said. "You told me it's where you were hiding when you blended into the fence."

There was a long silence. Imani took a step back. "How—how do you know that?" she finally said.

"You told me. How else could I know a small detail like that?"

"But I've never met you. I only got around to hanging up the bird feeder a week ago. How'd you know when I made it?" Her voice wavered.

Diana looked at Imani's expression—she was still doubtful, but she was looking at Diana differently now. *Maybe* she was finally getting through to her.

"I know it's all so confusing," Diana said carefully. "I get it. But the situation is really urgent, and the people outside are there to protect you, but their powers are diminished."

"Those people hanging out at the unfinished home?" Imani said. "I thought they were working on one of the sites."

"They're here to protect you. But I'm afraid once the guards bring the backup crew, they won't be enough to keep you safe."

Imani looked at her, debating, when a noise thundered from above. Imani gasped and gripped Diana's arm.

"Did you say the green thing came down my chimney?"

"Yes . . ."

With a trembling hand, Imani pointed to the fireplace.

Soot and dust tumbled to the floor, coating the cream carpet below. A loud noise rumbled outside the front of the house.

Diana raced toward the front window. They were there. An enormous white vehicle careened onto the driveway. The doors swung open, and ten people emerged. All of them wore the same uniform, black with a yellow feather. The god squad out front sprinted toward them. Within seconds, the two who'd been keeping watch in the back joined them. Three men and a woman. All four squared their shoulders, readying to fight.

Diana glanced back at the chimney. It continued shaking.

"They're too big to get through it. It's way too narrow," Diana said.

As though on cue, a high-pitched scream echoed from the chimney.

"We should go out the back way," Diana said.

"I don't—" Imani started to speak. But then there was a loud crash. Imani dropped the glowing rectangular tablet. Her face went pale.

"The sound came from upstairs, didn't it?" Diana said in a hushed voice.

"Definitely."

Heavy footsteps sounded above. The floorboards creaked loudly.

"We have to go." Diana rushed to the sliding door and opened it. The coast was clear. For now.

Imani stood frozen on the spot.

"Imani, please trust me," Diana pleaded. "I know it's a huge thing to ask of you because you don't remember me, but we don't have a second to spare."

The chimney shook. Bricks collapsed to the floor. Two guards tumbled into the main room covered in ash and soot. They weren't moving. But their chests rose and fell. They were alive. They could wake any second.

"Okay," Imani said shakily. "Yeah. Let's go."

Diana raced outside into the yard, stumbling into the greenery, Imani fast at her heels. She unlatched the gate. And then they sprinted toward the wooded forest.

Chapter Fifteen

"This way," Imani said breathlessly as they neared the tree line. "We'll follow the stream. It'll take us straight to a—"

"Got them!" a voice called out in the distance.

The guards. Imani and Diana picked up their pace. The terrain was uneven. Diana kept shifting her gaze to the ground so as not to lose her footing. Unruly ivy grew underfoot, and, beneath it, thick roots from nearby oaks and poplars alongside granite boulders poked through the dirt. Diana glanced back. Their pursuers were still in the distance but gaining quickly. Her knees burned as they scraped against her pants as she raced forward. *Don't lose pace with Imani,* Diana kept reminding herself. Her friend's gait was slower than Diana's, and she could not be left behind.

"They're catching up to us," Imani panted. "We can't outrun them."

We can do it, Diana wanted to respond, but the more they raced, the more Diana realized Imani was right. They hadn't lost their tail in the slightest. How long could they possibly run?

"I think we need to stop," Diana breathed out.

"And give up?" Imani glanced at her incredulously.

"No. We need to fight them."

"Fight them. You're kidding, right?"

Diana slowed down. She tried catching her breath. Her mind was racing. She didn't want to fight them. No part of her wanted to. But if they couldn't outrun them—what else could they do?

"I have a sword. And the Lasso of Truth," she told her. "If we can subdue them, then we can continue on safely."

"I c-can't. I don't know how to fight." Imani glanced furtively at the guards. They were still a short distance away but gaining on them.

"You don't need to fight," Diana reassured her. She pulled her sword from her belt. "Get behind me. Press your back against mine. Stick as close to me as possible. I've done something like this before with my friend Sakina. It's stressful, but it worked."

The guards were hopping over fallen branches and slicing vines from nearby trees. They were getting closer; they'd be here soon. Breathing heavily, Diana pulled out her lasso. She swallowed the fear that was rising up like bile. She'd been outnumbered before and she'd won. Diana gritted her teeth. There were three of them total. She'd try to loop them in with the lasso. It would be tricky to loop three men with one lasso, but it was worth a shot, because if she could manage it, they'd have to stop. And she'd have the sword as backup after that.

Diana angled one leg back, readying herself in a crouched position, when her back leg wobbled. Her foot caught—it snagged against something. Diana tried to straighten, but instead she tumbled backward. A snake hole, Diana realized when she saw the dark space among the ivy. She'd missed it, hidden as it was beneath the vines. Grunting, she yanked her foot out. Rising to her knees, she trembled. They were almost here. *I can still do this,* Diana thought. Steadily, she rose. *There's still time.*

"Wait!" Imani cried out. She stared at Diana with unmasked horror. Her expression grew ghostly pale.

"Imani, what—" But before Diana could say more, Imani leapt on top of her and tackled her to the ground.

Diana felt the wind knocked out of her as she fell backward. Imani pressed an arm against Diana's torso with all her strength.

"Imani. What are you doing?" she asked.

"Shh!" Imani whispered frantically.

The world grew hazy. A throbbing sensation filled Diana's entire body. Looking up, she felt sick. The guards were here. An arm's distance apart. Their hands were on their hips. It was no use trying to flee now, Diana thought miserably. They were on the ground, ready to be taken as easily as plucking flowers from a field. She braced herself. Seconds ticked by. Why hadn't the guards grabbed them yet? she wondered. They simply had to lean down and grasp her arm. Right then, one of them looked straight down at her. Diana met his bright blue eyes. Her mouth felt dry like sandpaper. But as quickly as he'd looked at her, he turned away.

"They were *right* here!" one of them grumbled. "I saw them plain as day!"

"I checked the underbrush. The trees. There's no sign of them," said another.

"Well, they've got to be here *somewhere*!"

"I think they went left," one of them said. "Toward the neighborhood."

They stomped about, their feet crunching against fallen dried leaves. A branch snapped loudly in the distance.

"There we go!" one of them cried. "They're thataway! I knew it!"

The three of them took off running.

Diana and Imani stayed completely still until all trace of footsteps and voices vanished. Soon the sound of birds overhead and squirrels scampering up trees filled the air again.

"They're gone," Diana whispered.

Imani released her. The throbbing sensation vanished. Diana sat up. Loose, damp grass from the forest floor was stuck to her pants, and her cream shirt was stained with earth. She looked over at Imani.

"You . . . you did it," Diana said slowly. Imani had activated her ability to blend, and she'd drawn Diana in, concealing them both. Diana moved to say something else to Imani, but she paused. Imani sat on the ground, trembling like a leaf.

"Oh, Imani," Diana began.

"Diana," Imani croaked out. "I remember."

CHAPTER SIXTEEN

Diana scooted next to Imani. Tears flowed from the girl's eyes, dripping down her cheeks.

"No." Imani shook her head. "This can't be right." She squeezed her eyes shut. "It has to be a dream. I'm cracking under the pressure. It—" Her voice broke off.

"Imani," Diana said urgently. "I know this is a lot. It's okay. Take a deep breath."

"No, it's not okay. All the memories," Imani burst out. "They're coming back to me. They're hitting me all at once. You were right. It's true. All of it. It's really true."

She shivered, wrapping her arms around her

knees. Diana was glad Imani's memories had unlocked somehow; she remembered. But processing so much all at once? Diana looked around nervously—the guards could be back any minute now.

"I can camouflage," Imani whispered. "A few days ago a green-cloaked thing really did dive down my chimney. It chased me all over the house and tried to kidnap me. And you were right. I blended into the fence right behind the bird feeder exactly like you said. It gave up after a while and went away. Then this lady appeared."

"Artemis," Diana said. "She's a goddess."

"She took me to a conjured island in a chariot flown by stags. And I met some people who were questioning me. Or gods, I guess. And Zeus was my . . . father? I remember being in a cage in a creepy place with skeletons, and spooky guards, and . . . you." She looked at Diana as though seeing her for the first time. "You were there. By my side. You tried to comfort me. And later, you saved me."

"We saved each other," Diana told her.

"I can't believe I did that. From out of nowhere." Imani shook her head in disbelief. "When they were gaining on us, and you slipped, something inside me snapped. It's like instinct took over. My body did what *I* didn't even *know* I could do. How did I just *do* that?"

"I don't know much about how powers work, especially ones that are locked away," Diana said. "But it sounds like the high stress unlocked your memories and power."

"But how could I forget something so huge?"

"When a god blocks your memories and sets your powers to dormant, it's hard to override it," Diana said gently. "But you never lost those powers or your memories. They were always within you. A part of you. Now they've returned once more."

"So now what?" Imani asked. The woods were empty, save the birds fluttering above. "They're looking for us. They could be back any second. Where do I go? It's not safe to go back home. They know where I live. And my mom's doing an overnight shift at the hospital. I could call her. Or maybe my aunt . . ." She groaned. "Except I left my phone at home."

"Is there an authority of some kind we can alert to the situation?" Diana asked. "Maybe they could help us."

"You mean the police?" Imani shook her head. "No way. Trust me. Telling them there are goons after us who want to turn us over to an evil genius who wants to take over the world?"

"He's definitely evil. But I'm not sure he's a genius," Diana said slowly, remembering his strange, elaborate costume and the way he cackled. "I saw him earlier today. Or at least a hologram of him. He's definitely somewhere here. I could describe him. Maybe they could help me retrace my steps."

"They won't believe us. Even I didn't believe you, remember?"

"Then I'll figure out a way to keep you safe," Diana promised. She rose to her feet and placed her hands on her hips. "But first, do you know how to get to the Exodus tower? The children are being held captive there."

"The Exodus tower?" Imani repeated.

"Have you heard of it?" Diana asked, hopefully.

"Um. Yeah. It's only one of the tallest buildings in the city."

"Is it nearby?"

"It's not walkable by foot, but we can probably make it there. MARTA isn't far from my house."

"Can we trust her to be discreet?"

"Her?" Imani repeated. "Oh—MARTA isn't a person; it's the city train. It should be able to drop us off close enough to the building."

"Great!" If Imani trusted this method of transport, it was the best shot they had. Once she helped guide Diana to the building, Diana would need to figure out where Imani could stay safe. She could not risk her friend getting caught. But she'd figure it out once they'd gotten there, Diana reminded herself. If she thought too far ahead, she'd risk getting frozen right where she was.

"Let's get going, then," Diana said. "The sooner the better."

"Before we go," Imani said, "um. We have to talk about your clothes."

"I know, it's not the best outfit considering how hot it is," Diana said. "The scarf in this heat *was* a bit much."

"No, it's not that," Imani said. "They're completely stained and messy. The jeans are ripped, and not in a good way."

She looked down, and, indeed, her pants were torn at the knees. Her cream-colored shirt was smeared with dirt. She was definitely going to draw attention looking this way.

"Well, I do have my other outfit," she said. Quickly, she pulled out her outfit from Themyscira and changed into it.

"What do you think?" She smoothed out her tunic with her hand. It had wrinkled a bit in the backpack, but after putting it on, Diana instantly felt at ease.

"Not sure it'll help you fit in," Imani said. "But at least you don't look like you need immediate medical attention."

"Shall we?" Diana said.

"The station's in that direction." Imani pointed

straight. "On the other side of the woods. Won't take but a few minutes."

"Good," Diana said with relief.

But before they could run, they heard a voice cry out in the woods.

"Diana. Is that *you*?"

Chapter Seventeen

Slowly, Diana turned around. The god squad. They were here. All four of them. The man and woman pretending to picnic in the back of the home. The two men she'd seen lingering out front. They hurried toward the girls.

"Imani," the woman exhaled. Her skin was pale, and her hair was pure white, like the snow of Targs. "Thank the gods. We've been worried sick about you. Diana, how in heavens have you ended up *here,* of all places?"

"And fleeing just now!" one of the men burst out. He ran a hand through his hair in exasperation. "We were beside ourselves."

"We *had* to get out," Diana said. "They were *in* the house!"

"That's what we're here for," one of the men said. He hurried toward her and stumbled on a vine. His eyes widened as he face-planted onto the ground.

"Are—are you okay?" Diana asked.

"Oh—yeah—I'm fine." He scrambled to rise. His face darkened into a red blush as he rose unsteadily. "A little clumsier lately. Coordination is off. Depth perception. Not sure what it is, but Zumius has got to be behind it somehow. Once things go back to the way they were, it'll be okay."

"Even though we're not at our top game, it doesn't mean we can't protect you," the pale woman reassured them. "We're your defenders, first and foremost."

Diana looked at their eager and determined faces and bit her lip. Convincing them to let them do what they needed to do wasn't going to be easy. This much was clear.

"Where are my manners? Princess Diana, my

name is Shaina," the woman said, bowing her head with respect. "It's an honor to meet you."

"I'm Phillip," the man next to her said. "These here are Anand and Viktor." He nodded to the other two. "We'll send word at once to your mother that we've located you."

"Phillip, any update since the last message we sent?" Shaina asked.

"Didn't go through." He sighed.

"Are the powers of the gods still snagging?" Diana asked.

"Unfortunately, it's only getting worse," Shaina said grimly.

"The worse their powers get, the worse ours do. Zumius's guards getting into the chimney and up the back of the house?" Viktor sighed. "Never would have happened if our powers were fully intact—we would've grabbed them well before then. We couldn't even get our safety barrier running properly around the perimeter of the house. It's shameful. The lapses are getting bad. We managed to tie up a good five of them back at your home, Imani, but three are still on the loose."

"But no need to fear!" Shaina said brightly. "We're here now. That's what matters. You're safe with us, and we'll get you home."

"I appreciate it," Diana said. "But Zumius is *here.* He's got the kids at the—"

"Wait. Are you saying Zumius, the one who tanked the powers of the gods and turned the universe into chaos, is somewhere here in the mortal world?" Viktor said with a raised eyebrow.

"Yes," replied Diana.

The god squad looked at one another silently. Then they chuckled.

Diana frowned.

"Oh, heavens, we're not laughing at *you,* dear," Shaina said quickly. "But the *mortal* world? There's no possible way."

"Well, it *is* possible," Diana responded. Even if they weren't making fun of her, they clearly didn't believe her. "I saw him."

"Diana," Anand said. He exchanged a glance with

the others. "We believe someone claimed to be Zumius. Likely to throw you off the trail."

"Fine." Diana dug her toe into the dirt. "I'll go and see for myself, then."

"I'm afraid you can't leave on your own." Viktor walked toward them. "Our orders are to protect the children. We can't let you go off wandering through the mortal world. Anything could happen."

"Viktor is right." Shaina nodded firmly. "*If* Zumius is here, all the more reason to be worried for your safety."

Diana stared at them. After *everything* she'd been through, she still had to explain herself? She still had to push against forced protection from those who thought they knew better? She would not hide until some sort of hypothetical help arrived. She had to help the children as soon as possible. There was not a moment to lose.

But . . . Diana glanced at Imani. She gripped her elbows together as though hugging herself. She hadn't said a word in all this time. She still looked shocked, having processed so many memories all in one breath. To undertake such a dangerous journey moments after Imani's monumental transition . . . it wasn't fair to her.

"I know you mean well," Diana told them. "But Zumius combed the worlds searching for me. He won't give up until he finds me, especially when I'm in his own backyard. He won't kill me. I know it as surely as I know my own name. But you all are in danger. While I search for the children, Imani should go with you."

"Excuse me?" Imani looked up.

"They are right, Imani. It *is* dangerous," Diana said. "I met Zumius earlier, and he's terrifying. No need for both of us to put our lives at risk. If you can tell me how to get to the tower, I can be on my way."

Imani looked at Diana and tilted her head. "Look, no offense, but I'm the reason those henchmen didn't find us. I'm not leaving you. Not going to happen."

It was true. Imani *had* helped them in a time of danger. Were it not for Imani, who knows what would have happened to them?

"I just . . . I worry," Diana said. "He's got guards. Lots of them."

"I get it." Imani nodded. "I'm more than a little bit freaked out. But we made it through the Underworld together and we did it again now. We evaded those guards, didn't we? We did it together. We'll do it together again."

"Uh . . ." Shaina's eyebrows threaded together. "Sorry to interrupt this sweet exchange, but *neither* of you is going to be chasing anybody. How about we get you to a hotel? It's a place where you can rent a room with a shower and a bed, and you can order some food to eat. I think a warm shower and some good food will do the trick, wouldn't it? You've both been through so much. You deserve a break."

She took a step toward them. Diana saw the glint of metal. Handcuffs. Viktor rested his hand nonchalantly upon a set of his own dangling from a loop on his belt. They were planning to bring them back no matter what, weren't they? Even if they refused. She was not going to let anyone dismiss her anymore simply because of her age. She had more than proven her competence and abilities.

"Or how about a compromise?" Diana offered. "You give us a few hours to find them. If we can't, we'll meet here at an agreed-upon time and we'll go with you wherever you want."

"Sorry, kids," Phillip said. "No negotiating. Appreciate your drive, but you'll need to come with us. Now."

Viktor drew his pair of handcuffs out.

"Are you *arresting* us?" Imani shrieked.

"I know. I'm sorry! We really don't want to," he apologized. "It's for your own safety. Truly."

Diana met Imani's gaze. Subtly, Imani nodded. "I'm sorry, too," Diana said. "We'll be sure to let Zeus know you tried your best. We'll make sure you don't get in trouble for this."

"Trouble for what?" Viktor moved toward them. "Diana. Wait a minute. Don't . . ."

But before he could finish his sentence, Imani and Diana were off. She knew the god squad meant well. They only wished to protect them. But too much was at stake—the future of the world was in the balance.

Chapter Eighteen

The girls raced as fast as they could.

"Imani! Diana! Wait!" the god squad cried out. They were fast, but not as fast as Zumius's guards.

"The MARTA should be that way!" Imani pointed straight ahead. "Once we hop on the train, we'll be safe."

"Girls! Come back! Please!"

Diana and Imani picked up their pace. The forest thinned now; the backs of homes were visible on either side of them. In the distance, Diana saw a metal bridge with vehicles snaking along a singular route. At last they stumbled onto a pavement filled with parked vehicles.

"Up—up there." Imani pointed to a platform,

wheezing. "Once we're inside, it'll take us to a stop a half block from the Exodus building."

The girls hurried toward the concrete pathway and the glass entrance doors ahead. Pushing against one, Diana frowned. The doors didn't budge.

"Shoot, I definitely did *not* think this through." Imani winced. "I don't have my pass. Doors won't open without a ticket."

Diana pressed her hands against the door again. The barrier bent the slightest bit against her gentle nudging. As she looked around, she saw that they were the only ones here. For now. She hated breaking rules, but the god squad had made it to the parking lot now. They'd be at the girls' heels within seconds.

Diana squared her shoulders. With all her strength, she pressed the doors apart as an enormous yellow vehicle pulled into the parking lot. Kids—dozens and dozens of them—burst out of the door. They wore matching clothing. Frazzled adults spoke over one another, attempting to corral them. The god squad stumbled, caught up in their chaos, tangled up with them. She had only a matter of seconds. Pressing harder, Diana squeezed her eyes shut and grunted. The gate inched open a crack. Then a bit more. It was a slim opening, barely room to slip sideways through. But it was enough.

"Hey!" A security guard hurried toward them. "What are you doing?"

"I'm sorry!" Diana shouted. They squeezed through the door and up the stairs. A train pulled in as they raced onto the platform. The doors beeped. People hurried out.

"Diana! Imani! Don't do it!" cried Phillip. He hurried up the steps. Sweat poured down his forehead. "This isn't safe!"

They hopped in as the doors began to shut. The train beeped before zooming off. Diana felt a wave of relief. But all solace vanished when she saw Imani's crestfallen face.

"Bad news," Imani said. "Looks like he made it on."

Diana squinted. In the distance, through a series of windows, she saw Phillip. He panted and glanced about. Then he looked directly at them.

"But he's in a different compartment," Diana said.

"I wish it were so simple."

Before she could elaborate, Diana saw for herself what the problem was. Phillip hurried toward a distant door, opened it, and slipped into the next car. He was going to hop through each one, Diana realized. He was making his way toward them on a moving train.

"We have to get out of here!" Diana said.

"We can't!" Imani gestured outside. The green landscape blurred around them before turning dark. The train sped forward underground. "We'll get off at the next stop."

But how soon would that be? The girls hurriedly pried open the door and hopped to the next train car. Wind whipped against Diana's hair, and the train felt shaky as they zipped through the darkness. They raced through into the next car, then the next. *When is this train going to stop?* Diana wondered frantically. She apologized as they bumped into suitcases and stepped on sneakers. They were in the last train car. This was it. Diana gathered her breath as she watched Phillip open another train car through the length of the train. Then the next. He was almost in their train car. Two more and he'd be there.

The train finally, suddenly, jerked to a stop. The doors blinked open. Imani moved to run, but Diana grabbed her elbow.

"Wait a sec," she said. "Let's get out when the timing is exactly right."

"Timing? Diana, he's almost here!"

Phillip opened the door to their car as passengers exited around Diana and Imani. He breathed heavily. He was steps away.

"Come on. Come on," Diana muttered, glancing at the train doors.

"Diana. Imani." Phillip moved toward them. He was within arm's reach now. "I—"

The train beeped. The doors began to tremble.

"Now!" Diana shouted.

The girls jumped out as the doors slammed shut. Diana's heart pounded when she looked back. The doors were sealed tight. The train beeped before bursting forward—with Phillip trapped inside. He banged his fists against a window, his face pressed against the glass as the train sped by with him inside.

"Whoa." Imani smiled. "Bye, Phillip."

"Are we anywhere near the building?" Diana asked once they reached the street. The scene before her felt dizzying. There were tall buildings all around them. Some seemed to stretch practically to the clouds. Vehicles zoomed past and lights blinked red, green, and yellow on street crossings.

"I'm not sure *where* we are." Imani frowned. Then she brightened. "Oh wait! A streetcar. I've been on one of those before. It has a stop not far from the building. Only issue is, we have no money. I don't know how I can blend onto that thing."

Diana watched the blue vehicle approach. "I have currency," she said. "Gold. Think they'll take it?"

"Let's hope so."

The driver peered at Diana suspiciously when she proffered the coin, but his eyes grew to the size of the coin itself when Diana held it out for him to examine.

Relieved, the girls sank into a back row as the

vehicle veered forward. Diana peered out the window as they rode through the city. Trees grew out of dirt patches set among concrete walkways. A gaggle of children no older than five clutched a thick rope as they walked with a woman who guided them toward a fenced play structure. She still couldn't wrap her mind around the fact that this place was why her mother had created Themyscira. Which meant her mother, too, had been on these lands. What exactly about this place had moved her mother to do so? she wondered. Ordinarily, she'd have longed to explore every nook and cranny, to linger more on this question, but for now, she had only one mission: find the children, break them free, and end Zumius's reign of terror.

Diana pressed a hand against the glass window of the streetcar and pushed back the exhaustion creeping up her spine. The gods had practically every power in the worlds at their fingertips, but they were rendered incapacitated by this roving hologram named Zumius. How could saving the fate of the world rest on their shoulders alone? The pressure was overwhelming. Diana swallowed. There was no use in feeling frustrated at their circumstances. All she could do was go forward and give it everything she had.

"This is our stop," Imani said as the streetcar braked.

Stepping out, the girls looked up at an enormous blue building with a slanted roof.

"Is that it?" Diana asked.

"That's an aquarium," Imani said. "The Exodus tower is behind it. We need to make our way around and—"

"Diana! Imani!" It was Viktor and Anand. They raced through a park across the street, flailing their hands frantically. "Please! Stop!"

"Let's hide out there." Diana pointed to the aquarium. "But, oh wait." She paused. "Do you have to pay to get in there, too?"

"I don't think we'll have time to convince them to take a gold coin. They're too close on our heels. Let's do it my way," Imani said. "Grab my hand. Maybe we can sneak into the building unnoticed."

"Can you move *and* stay hidden?" Diana asked her.

"No clue," Imani said. "But I think we'll have to take our chances and find out."

They raced to the edge of the building until they found an obscure spot hidden from view. The girls squeezed hands and pressed their backs against the wall. The throbbing feeling returned to Diana's body. The world grew hazy. The duo inched their way toward the entrance. Diana held her breath. She glanced around—but the underwater sensation remained—and no one so much as glanced their way. Two older women stood in the line to enter. They handed a ticket to an employee wearing a hat bearing the logo of an orange smiling fish. He clicked it through a machine and waved them inside.

Diana and Imani carefully slid past the ticket collector. It was the strangest thing to see the world plain as day, but to walk past everyone unnoticed. The girls were almost through the opened door when the god squad raced forward. They tried sliding past the employee, but he held up a hand, stopping them.

"Tickets, please," he said in a dispassionate voice.

"Oh, we'll only be a minute," Anand said quickly. "We think a pair of children headed in here a little while earlier. We need to get them as soon as possible. It's not safe."

"What exactly are you saying? No one can just *wander* in." The employee sounded peeved. "That's what I'm here for."

"You may not have seen them," Anand said. "They—"

"Excuse me?" The ticket collector's expression reddened. "Not seen them? So you really *are* implying I negligently left my spot?"

"No!" Viktor exclaimed. "That's not what—"

"No children came through unaccompanied," he said, frowning. "If you'd like to visit the premises, buy a ticket from the window. Though I warn you there's only an hour until closing."

The two men stared at the ticket collector, and Diana's stomach clenched—but then Diana felt relieved as Anand and Viktor doubled back the way they came.

Inching toward the entrance to the exhibits, Diana felt cool air against her face. They were in.

Diana and Imani edged their way up the steps, keeping their bodies pressed flush against the wall to maintain their cover. They slid past a glass tank of translucent jellyfish bobbing in the water. An open tank of stingrays. Children squealed and clapped. At last the two girls found a spot upstairs in an empty room. They stayed still against the wall, waiting, not daring to say a word. Had they successfully thrown them off the trail?

At last, the crowds emptied out. The aquarium closed. Diana watched a bored-looking security cop make the first of her rounds. As soon as she left, Imani released Diana.

"That was the longest I've ever stayed hidden," Imani whispered. "Wow."

"Was it difficult?" Diana asked.

"No. Just weird," Imani said. "But it's good to know I can blend longer than I'd realized."

Diana was grateful Imani had stuck it out with

her. She hated putting someone else at risk with this mission, but her help was invaluable.

"There it is." Imani pointed out a window. "The Exodus tower."

Diana looked out. It was an enormous steel building jutting straight into the sky. Taller than any of the others she'd seen. Red lights blinked atop. The tower was divided into roughly three parts. A large base, a narrower middle, and a thinner top with a huge metal balcony all around it—like an observation deck. Up there were the kids, hooked up to the Splectra. Zumius was probably there, too. Diana pressed her hand against the glass. She ached to get there as soon as possible, but they had to plan this out. There could be no mistakes.

They headed down the stairs and through a glass tunnel, and Diana's breath caught as she looked around. Fish of all colors swam above them, around them. Despite how much weighed on her mind, Diana couldn't help but be mesmerized by the sight.

"This aquarium is pretty huge," Diana said quietly, hoping not to attract the attention of the security guard. "Think there might be a back exit door we could take? Viktor and Anand are probably waiting for us to come out. If we could find some other exit, it might be safer."

"Those dark doors up ahead say Exit—hopefully they're unlocked from the inside."

"We can try," Diana said.

"Well, one question . . ." Imani glanced at her. Fish swept across the water atop their heads. "Do we have a plan on *how* to get the kids out once we get to Exodus? I assume Zumius will have measures in place to stop people like us from waltzing in and grabbing them."

"I don't know exactly how to get them out yet, especially because we have no idea what sort of blockades he's got in place," Diana admitted. "I think if I tried to plan ahead for something as unpredictable and out of our control as this, I'd freeze up and do nothing at all. So far we've managed to make it by handling whatever comes our way when it comes. There's no other way for situations like this. The good thing is, the kids have special abilities like you.

Lumierna bends metal. Aiko bends minds—she can control others without moving a muscle. And Aristaeus can harness the wind. Bees, too. Once we're all together, Zumius won't stand a chance."

"I hope so," Imani said.

A loud splash sounded from above.

"What was that?" Imani frowned.

Diana moved to respond, but before she could, she heard a voice.

"Diana!"

Another loud splash. Looking up she grew still. Viktor. He was in the water, swimming toward her. His arms paddled furiously as he approached the glass window separating them. He tapped his fingers against the tank. He was trying to reach her through the glass, Diana realized.

"No!" Diana waved her arms and shook her head furiously. "Go back." She motioned with her hands.

"We're coming to get you!" another voice cried out.

There was a splash. Anand. He, too, swam toward them and beat his fists against the glass.

What were they doing? Diana stared at them. Quickly, the two men turned away, as though to swim back up, but instead, their bodies slowly grew limp.

"They don't look good," Imani said.

They *weren't* good, Diana realized. They were drowning.

CHAPTER NINETEEN

Diana's heart pounded. She had to help them. They would die if she didn't. But how? She couldn't exactly break the glass—it would spell the end for all the marine life within.

"Stairs?" Diana glanced about. Had a guard noticed yet? If not, someone would soon enough. "There's gotta be a way up!"

Racing out of the tunnel, Diana scanned the floor-to-ceiling glass room for a door until at last she spotted one. She pressed it open, and she and Imani charged up the steps and into a wide room with an open tank of water. Diana inhaled and dove straight in. She propelled past angelfish and a school of groupers toward Viktor's and Anand's limp bodies floating in the water.

Please be okay, she thought frantically. She swept down and grabbed them by their collars and, yanking firmly, swam toward the surface. At last, Diana lifted them out of the tank, rolling them onto the rubber-matted floor.

Viktor's eyes fluttered open. He gasped for air. Anand flipped to his side and coughed out water.

"Oh my gods," Anand panted. "I thought . . . I thought that was . . . I thought that was it."

Water dripped down Diana's hair. She was soaked. But it was worth it. They were all right.

"You saved our lives," Anand said.

"We broke into pairs to look for you," Viktor panted. "We thought you might come here, since it's a clear shot from the Exodus tower . . . and then . . . when I saw you below, I thought you'd fallen in. That worked out great, didn't it?"

"It's like you said," Diana told them gently. "Whatever the cause might be, your abilities are affected here in unexpected ways."

"Not sure mere gratitude suffices for saving our

lives." He rose unsteadily. "But thank you all the same."

"I know you came here to help us," Diana said. "But you can see now we don't need babysitting, right? We can take care of ourselves."

"Diana. Imani. Try to see this from our perspective," Anand said, wheezing as he steadied himself to a seated position. "I realize we're not at our full capacity. But let's say Zumius is really up there. And let's say the children are there, too. We can't let you head into the devil's lair. Zeus would never allow it. You know this as well as we do."

"Tell Zeus to come, then." Diana folded her arms. "We'd welcome the help."

"We—we can't reach him." Anand hung his head. "It's been nearly two days."

"Then let us go. We need to do this."

Anand and Viktor looked at each other.

"We'll go with you," Viktor finally said. "If they're up there, you could use a hand, couldn't you?"

"Uh . . ." Imani glanced at Diana. "Well—"

Diana knew what she was thinking. Anand and Viktor had nearly drowned trying to give the girls "a hand"! The god squad meant well, but with their skills so affected, they were vulnerable.

"Zumius's guards. They could kill you. But they don't want to harm us," Diana said. "It's our saving grace. It's why we can take this risk."

"We won't be able to live with ourselves if anything happens to you," Viktor said. "We took an oath."

"Keep sending word to the gods," Diana said as the four of them carefully exited the building through a back door—taking care to avoid the security guard on her rounds. They hurried onto the pavement outside. Vehicles sped past them on the road. "You're the only ones with any chance of reaching them. If they can help us, we more than welcome it."

Diana paused. Her eyes widened. In the distance, hurrying down the pavement toward them, were three men in all-black clothing with the signature yellow feather.

"The guards!" Diana shouted. "They found us."

Viktor and Anand looked at each other.

"Three on two?" Viktor asked.

"I like those odds," Anand said with a nod to the girls. "We'll fend them off while you run. Be quick and *please* stay safe."

"Stop!" the guards called out. "Get back here! Now!"

The girls ran as cars driving by them squealed to a stop. People poked their heads out to stare, and parents pushing strollers paused to gape at the strangely costumed men. Glancing back, Viktor and Anand stood in fighting position as the guards grew closer. Diana hesitated. Would this duo really be able to take on Zumius's guards?

"What are you waiting for?" Viktor shouted to the girls. "Go! Now! We got this!"

The guards moved to get around the god squad, but true to their word, Viktor and Anand blocked them. The guards swung their fists, but Anand and Viktor deftly swerved and roundhouse-kicked them square in their chests, sending the three guards—and themselves—tumbling backward.

Diana and Imani raced down the street as a

piercing alarm blared. A black-and-white vehicle with red and blue flashing lights zipped by them, toward the fighting.

"Here!" Imani called out. She opened the door to a café. The girls rushed inside. They settled down on stools overlooking tinted windows and tried to catch their breath. People around them drank coffee and chatted in hushed voices. Soothing music played overhead.

"A different kind of blending in," Imani said. She wiped her hand against her forehead. "We can stay here until we figure out what we're going to do next because we've arrived." She nodded toward the window.

Looking outside, Diana forgot to breathe for a moment. There it was. An enormous steel building across the street. Armed guards stood outside. They wore the black-and-yellow uniform and dark sunglasses.

From this vantage point the Exodus tower felt even larger than before. She looked at the guards. The full reality of what she and Imani would have to do hit her. She'd have to figure out how to get past them. How to get up the building.

And not get caught.

Music played softly overhead. She watched the other patrons drink teas and coffees as they read books. Or spoke to one another in hushed voices. Heaviness settled over Diana as the weight of her responsibility sank into her like stones. These people had no idea how fragile the peace of the world was at this very moment. How much was at stake. Zumius didn't just threaten the gods, or the children up in that building—he was a danger to everyone. He had to be stopped.

Chapter Twenty

A few hours passed as the girls sat in the café trying to come up with a plan. The line to order a drink was now snaking out the door. Three men sat across from them on leather sofas, speaking in quiet voices. Two kids around Diana's age hovered over a device while sipping from enormous steaming mugs. Diana and Imani had no money to buy a drink, but luckily the cashier took one of Diana's Targuni coins and handed the girls sandwiches and drinks. Diana had no appetite, and she was bone tired, but she forced herself to eat—she knew she'd need the strength.

Diana looked at the different concoctions people sipped. Steam rose from many cups. But neither

her food, nor what the other people were consuming, was anything like the fresh meals she enjoyed back home. Thinking of home made her ache. She needed to rescue the children and take down Zumius once and for all.

Diana eyed the building again, and the guards. There were ten of them in total. Their jaws were set tensely. They scarcely moved from their posts. She *needed* a plan. They'd agreed to wait until nightfall to conceal themselves under cover of darkness as best as they could, but how exactly were they going to get past these men?

"Could we use your powers to get by them?" Diana asked Imani.

"Maybe," Imani said, hesitating. "But it'll require a lot of maneuvering. It's at least two hundred steps away and I'm not sure *what* I'd blend into to get there. The street? Plus we'd have to open the door without them noticing."

A flash of light within the building caught Diana's eye. A red beam.

"Are those lasers?" Diana asked.

Imani craned her head forward. "I guess so." She

nodded grimly. "No idea if my blending can fool lasers."

"The whole thing is probably booby-trapped," Diana said. Her chest constricted. How many obstacles lay in store for them?

She examined the sides of the tower as the sky darkened outside. The tower began blocky and wide, narrowing to the top, where a circular balcony surrounded the top floor. The windows appeared dark. There were thick trusses and ample window ledges lining the first third of the tower. So long as no one was peeking through the windows, this bit would be easy enough to climb. But as the building rose, it got trickier; the trusses gave way to sleek windows, pressed flat against the building. Higher up the construction shifted again, though from where she sat, it was hard to make out just how much. It seemed scalable. Maybe. But even if it was something Diana herself could climb, what about Imani? It wasn't like Diana could make her way to the top of an eighty-story building and throw down a vine from a nearby tree to help Imani climb up, like she'd done for her friends when she scaled the granite cliff of Sáz.

A woman's crackly voice boomed into the room. "The café is closing in five minutes."

When they stepped onto the street, Diana felt a tap on her shoulder. Diana flinched. Had they found her this quickly? She grazed the hilt of her sword with her hand, steeling herself, but when she turned around, she frowned. They weren't guards. They were the two kids she'd seen earlier in the coffee shop.

"It *is* you!" The girl turned to the boy she was with.

"Told you, didn't I?" The boy grinned triumphantly.

"Wow!" The girl's jaw dropped in shock. "This is so cool."

"You were *amazing*!"

"Um, I think you have the wrong person," Diana said.

"You rescued the girl from the monkey bars, didn't you? I recognized your cool outfit."

"How do you know about that?" Diana asked. "Were you there?"

"We saw the video. *Everyone's* seen it," the girl

gushed. She held up her device. There was a shifting of green grass—a blur—and then there was Diana; she swooped in, grabbing Fiona before she hit the ground. Someone had captured the moment. *How is this possible?* Diana stared at the image as it played and replayed. She wanted to wave it away as a trick of the eyes, except it was *her.* The blur in the image was Diana. She'd known she could run fast, but seeing herself doing it . . . it was far faster than she'd realized. In this video, she was . . . impossibly fast.

"You've gone viral!" the boy exclaimed. "My sister's gonna flip when I tell her I met you."

"Was it Photoshopped?" the girl asked. "You can tell me. I won't tell anyone if it was."

Photoshopped? Diana blinked. "I saw the girl. She was about to fall, and I wanted to make sure she didn't get hurt."

"Can you sign my backpack?" The boy handed her a marker.

"What?" Diana raised an eyebrow.

"Yeah, if you don't mind. Not every day you meet an actual honest-to-goodness celebrity!"

Diana stifled a laugh. She wrote her name on the

fabric and watched the duo excitedly hurry away. The mortal world was a strange one.

Taking care not to get recognized again, Imani and Diana hurried alongside the other exiting customers until they reached an alleyway next to the Exodus tower. After slipping in, they waited. An hour passed as night settled thick around them. The crowds thinned.

Diana looked up and swallowed. The moon above them was obscured by clouds. Dark, unsettling ones promising rain, she feared. She inched to the edge of the building and peered at the guards out front. It'd been hours since she'd first seen them from the coffee shop. No one had moved positions. Despite the inky night, they still wore sunglasses. *Are they not human?* Diana wondered. Maybe they were automatons, like she'd seen on the conjured land of the gods.

Diana glanced at the tower walls. She didn't want to do this. No part of her did. She pressed her palm against the building and traced the lower trusses with her fingers. They were thick and sturdy. At least there was that.

"Oh no." Imani shook her head. "Don't tell me you're thinking of *climbing* up the skyscraper."

"We have to talk out all our options."

"This building is ridiculously high. It's impossible. I'd rather take my chances trying to go *through* the building."

Diana understood Imani's hesitation. She didn't want to consider making her way up a skyscraper. But she did know they needed to reach the kids. And if they couldn't get past the guards, they had to find another way.

And this right here was the only other way.

Chapter Twenty-One

Diana and Imani edged down the alley and made two right turns until they were on the other side of the building. Diana glanced up at the sky and bit her lip. It would be hard enough to make this climb in *any* circumstances, but if it rained? It would make it practically impossible.

"Listen," Imani said. "You need to really think this plan through. You're strong, no one doubts it for a second. But you're not a mountain climber, much less a building climber!"

"I'm not," Diana said. "But I have scaled some pretty steep things."

"As high as an eighty-story tower?"

"Not exactly." She thought of the cliff she'd scaled

on the nation of Sáz. It had been a flat granite ledge shooting straight up about a thousand feet. There had hardly been a crack within the surface to get a toehold in, but even then, despite how perilous it was, she had managed to make it all the way up. She had found a way.

And even though this building was enormous, jutting into the dark clouds, it *had* footholds and plenty of places to grab on to. Where the two girls stood, decorative trusses stuck out almost like narrow stairs and went up to Diana's knees. Above that, the bottom third of the building had wide window ledges to balance on between climbing. So long as no one spotted them, and so long as the rain held off long enough, she could do it. Farther up, it looked trickier as the building narrowed and narrowed, but they'd figure it out as they climbed. They'd have to.

But as she glanced back at Imani's uncertain face, the same concern returned. What about Imani?

"I think we need to look for a place for you to hide out," Diana said. "Somewhere out of sight while I get up this thing."

"Diana!" Imani exclaimed. "No way."

A streak of lightning lit up the sky, and thunder rolled in the distance. Diana paused. A flicker of hope lit within her. Was that Zeus? Was he trying to reach them? If it was actually Zeus, she could tell him where the children were and he'd take care of the rest. She glanced nervously at the sky, waiting. Another shot of lightning burst in the distance, but no god appeared. Diana pushed back her disappointment. Perhaps he *was* trying to find them—perhaps the lightning meant he was close by—but they couldn't wait to see; she had to act now.

"One slip and you'll meet your end," Imani said nervously. "Let's figure out a plan B. Together."

Diana tapped her fingers against her belt. Slowly, she looked down. The rope. *Of course.* Imani couldn't make the climb on her own. But there *was* a way Diana could help her.

"My lasso," Diana said. She grazed her hand over the rope. "That's how you'll get up this building with me."

"Not sure I'm following you." Imani raised an eyebrow.

"This building looks really complicated," Diana

said. "But we're both tall enough to jump from sill to sill so long as we grip the next window and hoist ourselves up. You can do it, Imani. I've seen you in the Underworld. You are cool and calm under pressure. The only thing is, this building is really high."

"Yep, the *only* thing," Imani retorted.

"This rope will connect us," Diana said. "You'll have one end tied to your waist, and I'll have the other end tied to mine. You *won't* fall. But if you do somehow lose your grip, I'll be able to stop it."

"*Or* we could both end up falling together to our ends."

"I won't let that happen," Diana told her firmly. "But we do have to move. The clouds don't look good. We need to be up there before it starts raining and our climb gets slippery. We've done so much. The kids are right up there. Once we set them free, we'll have a team so powerful nothing will stand a chance against us."

Diana unknotted her lasso and wrapped one end around Imani's waist before knotting the other end around herself. She yanked at both their knots.

"See?" she said. "The grip is solid. We can do it."

She hoped she sounded more confident than she felt.

Imani looked down at the rope. "Okay," she said grimly. "Let's do it."

They walked up to the building, and Diana pressed a hand against its smooth exterior. She tested out the first beam. It was narrow but sturdy. Pressing her toes into each step, she kept her balance.

"Follow along as I go," Diana told her. "From here, I'm going to jump up and grab the window ledge above. Do what I do. I'll tell you what's coming next and how to prepare for it. The biggest thing to remember is no matter what, don't let go of whatever you're gripping until you've got one of your arms or legs firmly on the next part."

Jumping to the window ledge above them was easy enough. Diana stretched out onto her tiptoes and, with her fingers, grasped the ledge while pressing her feet firmly against the thick decorative trusses. Grunting, she lifted herself up and stood firmly on the brick edge, bracing against the back of the building. She held her hand out for Imani and pulled her up.

Breathing shakily, Diana wondered if anyone would spot their climb up the building—this was something she hadn't thought about before. The windows were darkened, and blinds covered any view of the interior. Before them was another building, the one that had helped form the alleyway, but it also appeared to be vacant at this hour. Though she could hear the sounds of trains and vehicles not far from them, the alley was empty.

"That wasn't so bad," Imani said. She caught up to Diana and put her hands on her hips. "We're only five feet from the ground. But I still did better than I thought I would."

"The ledges are your friends. Keep a tight grip. It'll be like this for the next forty or so stories, but it'll *feel* scarier because we're going higher up."

"Let's get it over with, then."

They carefully made their way to the second ledge. Then the third. The fourth.

"Wow," Imani exhaled at the seventh floor. "We're doing it."

A fat raindrop landed on Diana's nose. Looking up, she saw that the clouds were dark but, thankfully, fast moving. Maybe they could luck out and the clouds would ferry along without pouring upon them. It could *not* rain. They could not do this climb with a slick surface.

Diana jumped to grip the next window. Farther and farther up they climbed. Each ledge was the same as the last, and Diana's fingers began to burn the higher they ascended. Her arms ached. It'd been at least an hour by now. But the smattering of raindrops hitting her now and again kept her focused.

Finally, they reached the last windowsill. After pulling Imani up, Diana looked at the street below. They were a third of the way up, and already the cars below were as tiny as insects. Imani kept her gaze fixed up.

"I'm not looking down. Not going to look," she whispered.

"This next bit is trickier," Diana said. She ran her palms over the smooth, dark windows. The building narrowed here, and the wind seemed to sway the tower. The glass was cut into rectangles the size of her body, but, thankfully, the edges jutted out the slightest bit where the panes were connected by metal. There was just enough space on the metal ledges between panes to grip onto them with her hands and press up against the glass by planting her feet in firmly. "I won't be able to pull you up for this leg of the climb," she told Imani. "You're going to have to shimmy up, digging your fingers against the gaps between the windows and using friction to climb up. Or, if you can, stick your foot in the gaps between the windows."

Diana gripped the edge of the windows and strained, climbing up. They made their way up the first window. Then the second. Diana's fingers pulsed with pain. The granite cliffs of Sáz were terrifying, but they didn't hold a candle to the danger she felt now. It had been one thing to climb up alone, and an entirely different matter to have Imani with her, laced to her by rope. She was directly responsible for Imani's fate. If she slipped or made any misstep, it was not only her own life at stake.

"We're halfway to the next part," Diana called out. "We—"

Her breath caught in her throat. Rain. It was officially sprinkling now. Thunder rumbled louder in the distance. Diana picked up her climbing pace.

At the next section of the building, the top third, Diana sighed and felt herself relax just the slightest bit. Beams—the rest of the building consisted of thick beams trickling all the way up to the balcony. They were almost there. They'd be up at the top in no time. Diana grabbed the first beam and heaved herself up. It was slick with raindrops, but wide enough to grip tight.

Diana climbed up the next beam. Then the third. With each passing second, more rain flicked against her body, trailing down her hair and her cheeks. Lightning reflected against the glass, followed instantly by thunder. They were almost to the top, and the storm was upon them in full force now. There was only one more step to climb before they reached the balcony.

"We're almost there!" Diana yelled to Imani, hoping to be heard over the roar of the pounding, intense rain. "Hang tight!"

"Okay! Because this rain is really— Oh!" Imani yelped. Diana moved to ask her what was wrong, but now she felt it. The rope against her waist went taut, dragging her backward. Imani! She'd lost her grip! Imani's body slammed against a glass window, her arms flailing. She swayed in the air, her eyes wide with terror.

"Hang on!" Diana called down to her. "I've got you!"

Diana squeezed her fingers and dug her toes into the beam's edges. Gravity seemed intent on shoving Diana down along with Imani.

"Grab the window!" Diana shouted.

"I can't! It's too slippery!"

"Yes, you can! Swing yourself toward it! You can do it!"

Imani kicked her legs toward the window. Rain was coming down harder and harder. Diana's feet slipped against the glass. She gripped the window's edge and bit her lip so hard that she tasted blood.

Looking down at Imani, she debated. Maybe if she held on with one hand and with the other reached down to pull on the rope to hold it steady, Imani could swing back to safety.

"I'm going to pull you closer," Diana cried out. "As soon as you—"

Diana gasped as a burst of wind blew violently over her and the building lurched in response.

Diana's hands slipped from the window.

Chapter Twenty-Two

Weightlessness filled Diana's body. She was falling. As Diana swam upward in vain, her heart caught in her throat. At any second, they'd hit the concrete below.

How could she meet her end *now*?

How could Zumius *win*?

How could she have taken Imani down with her?

Tears streamed down her face as she stuck her hands out in desperation, trying to grasp a solid edge. In a matter of moments, it would all be over. Both she and Imani would meet their end. All of this would have been for nothing.

"Diana!" Imani called out.

Diana opened her eyes and blinked. Imani was

below her, dangling as she'd been from the rope. But Diana *hadn't* fallen. She was levitating in midair; her hands were up and swimming frantically inches from the edge of the beam she'd slipped from. Diana gritted her teeth and, reaching up, she grasped onto a ledge. Hastily, she scrambled atop it and climbed onto the balcony. Looking around, she blinked. Was this a dream?

Shakily, Diana reached down and pulled Imani up. Panting, Imani stumbled onto the balcony's ledge. Luckily, it was wide enough for both girls to sit down and catch their breath. Diana exhaled. Thunder sounded above. Rain fell hard against them. But they'd made it. Imani was okay. She looked down at the distant earth below. The sensation of falling had felt so real. But had she imagined it? Or had she . . .

"Did I . . . ?" Diana paused, unsure how to ask Imani.

"Fly?" Imani said softly. "Yeah. You most definitely did."

Diana's mind raced. Zumius had said— But no. That was ridiculous. As she glanced at the night sky, the bolts of lightning in the distance—those streaks of yellow—were evidence clear as day that Zeus had intervened in Diana's moment of need. There was no other explanation.

"Whoa," Imani said under her breath. Diana followed her gaze to a window. There it was. Behind them, the place they'd been trying to reach. The room was enormous and all white, and there stood enormous shelves filled with books, stacks of papers, and vials of liquid.

Diana's breath caught. The machine. A black one shaped like a triangle, wide on one end and narrowing into a point on the other, was set in the center of the room. Buttons on it blinked green and red, and wires jutted out all over it. She saw the kids fanned out around it. Each of them was trapped in a glass box, restrained, with wires coming out of their arms and leading to the machine.

She pressed against the window. There had to be an opening. A way to break in.

Imani touched her arm. "The guards are there," she said. "By the entrance."

Quickly, the girls ducked below the window ledge and peered over. Indeed, the same sort of uniformed men paced the front of the room, their arms at their sides, brown nightsticks in their hands. Diana shivered. The air was cooler up here and whipped fast against her hair. The rain had eased, but thunder and lightning still shook the sky. After what felt like an eternity, the guards exited the room.

"We have to break in while they're gone," Diana said. She pushed against the windows, but they were sealed shut. Every moment that passed was critical. Thunder clanged again, and lightning shot into the darkness in the distance. Thunder! Diana's eyebrows shot up. That was it! Next time it thundered, she could smash a window without drawing attention.

They didn't have to wait long. One tense minute later, lightning flashed. Rattling thunder followed, crackling in the sky. Diana grabbed the hilt of her sword and, with a single swoop, jabbed it into the window, shattering the glass into a million pieces.

Chapter Twenty-Three

Diana peered into the room through the newly cracked window. The jagged edges of broken glass gleamed against the lightning in the background. Could thunder *really* mask the sound of breaking glass? She waited for someone to appear. For a figure to grab her. But so far, the coast seemed clear. She pushed at the jagged edges with the hilt of her sword and they crumpled to the ground. Gingerly, the girls hopped into the room. Thunder crackled. Gusts of wind swept into the room. They'd made it. They'd finally reached the kidnapped children! The significance of the moment hit her tenfold. She'd achieved the unachievable—she'd done the thing *no one* thought she could do on her own. She'd scaled a building to do it! But the momentary joy was undercut by what she saw before her.

Not one of the children had even looked over at the noise of the glass breaking. Diana had just taken a step toward them, when she bowled over and coughed. A foul odor overwhelmed the room.

"It smells like disinfectant." Imani scrunched her nose. "Like someone dumped a tractor-trailer full of it on the ground."

The black machine she'd seen from outside beeped loudly. Across from it, a bookshelf was filled with glass vials of all different colors.

Panting, Diana turned her attention to the kids, who were spread out like the legs of a spider around the Splectra. The kid who she assumed was Lumierna had hair that was cut short. They were double her size, and muscles bulged from their arms and legs. Aiko was lean and tall. Her dark hair was plaited into a braid, the tendrils loose and messy around her oval face. And the child she thought was Aristaeus had a ring of flowers on his head. None of them said a word. They weren't sleeping—their eyes were open—but they seemed to be in some kind of vegetative state.

Diana's eyes landed on two other enclosures sitting empty.

"They're for us, aren't they?" Imani said softly.

"Looks like it," Diana said. "But they won't get us in there. They won't."

"We thought the same thing," a voice spoke.

It was Lumierna. Their eyes were placid.

Diana raced toward them. "Thank the gods, you're okay. We have to get all of you out of here."

"Sure you will," Aiko replied. "You walked right into his nest, but you'll be the one to get us out?"

"I'm here to help you," Diana said.

"Diana's right," Imani said. "Together we can overtake this thing, whatever it is. Once we break you out, nothing can stop us."

"It's a nice idea," Aristaeus said. "But I've been here a while now. It's impossible to break out."

"He's right. . . ." Lumierna kept their gaze fixed on their lap. "I mean . . . what's the point?"

"What's the *point*?" Diana repeated dumbly.

Lumierna was tied up to a machine against their will, and they had no interest in breaking out?

This had to be Zumius's doing. He'd done something to them to cause them to react with such apathy. Maybe he was drugging the kids? Diana noted that the wires in their arms had what appeared to be magnets of some sort clipped around them. Were the wires causing the children to feel resigned to their fate? It was the only logical explanation.

Diana rushed to Aristaeus's side. She tugged at the glass handle of his enclosure. She forcefully yanked at it. Imani joined her. Their cheeks flushed from the effort, but—nothing. The door didn't so much as budge.

"Look," Aiko said, "whoever you are, it's sweet you want to help, but it's best to get out while you can."

"My name is Diana. Imani and I—we're here to get you out."

"Oh, *Diana*." Lumierna nodded. "We've heard about you. A *lot*."

"Look, here's the deal. I'll spare you the effort. Nothing works," Aiko said dully. Her voice echoed in the open space. "He'll get you. He always does. And those two empty seats, you'll both be in them soon enough. It's not a matter of *if.* It's a matter of *when.*"

Tears formed in Diana's eyes. These children were so powerful. And they'd given up?

"The wires," Imani whispered. "That must be what's making them this way."

Diana looked at the children. The wires snaked out of their enclosures and connected to the machine. Imani was right. How else would they let themselves be used as pawns in this being's scheme?

She drew her sword and hurried toward the machine.

"I'm going to cut the wires," Diana told Imani. "It might help."

"Diana! No! Don't cut them!"

Diana froze at the new voice. She blinked. It couldn't be.

"We're behind the bookshelf."

Sakina?

In a daze, she followed the sound of the voice. *I'm hearing things,* she thought. *I must be.* But as she walked behind the shelf, Diana felt the color draining from her face. It was Sakina. Her back was pressed against the wall. A gag dangled by her cheek.

And next to her—

"Augustus?" Diana said softly. He was still gagged. She hadn't seen him since the island of Sáz, when they had bid their farewells after destroying the demon who had hunted for her. Hurrying over, she ripped his gag off. He coughed and inhaled sharply.

"We meet again," he said with a small smile.

"You can't cut the wires," Sakina said urgently. "Whatever is going in and out of those kids, it's powerful. The kids said so themselves. I think yanking the wires out could put the kids into some sort of shock state."

"Sakina! What are you doing here?" Diana exclaimed.

"I could ask the same of both of you," Sakina

replied. “But I should have guessed you’d show up on your own terms. I’m so glad you’re okay.”

Augustus and Sakina seemed like themselves. They didn’t seem affected by any sort of charm. She looked at the other kids. It had to be the wires attached to the children making them this lethargic and despondent.

Looking back at Augustus and Sakina, she realized neither had come toward her. Moving closer, she saw why: thick rope bound their hands to a metal handle bolted into the wall.

“Yep,” Sakina nodded. “We’re a bit tied up at the moment.”

“Rope is easy enough to take care of.” Diana pulled out her sword and, with two slices, Sakina’s and Augustus’s restraints fell to the floor.

“Thanks.” Sakina rubbed her bruised wrists. “They didn’t have to bind us *that* tightly.”

“How did you end up here?” Imani asked.

“Zumius heard from Hades about my ability to speak to animals,” Sakina said. “He thought it could prove helpful to his mission.”

"From what I have been able to gather, word about my potion-making skills got out and Zumius decided I could also be useful," Augustus said. "I always wanted to be a renowned potion maker. G-guess I should've been careful what I wished for."

"We saw him today," Sakina added. "He's terrifying."

"We have to get everyone out of here as soon as possible," Diana said. "There's no telling when the guards will return."

"The kids won't do anything," Augustus said. "I can't be absolutely certain what it is he's given them to cause their apathy, but based on the scent when he administers it, I believe he's using a pazzo bean. It instills hopelessness in whoever imbibes it."

"Hopelessness," Diana said. "I had no idea you could inject someone with a feeling. How awful!"

"Yes, and at the doses he's injecting them," Augustus said, "they're so resigned to their fate they gave up before they even began trying."

Diana thought of the trees looming over the River Styx as she'd made her way to the Underworld. Just the one drop of liquid landing on her face had sent her into a haze of uncertainty and terror. She looked at the threesome—of all the people in the world, how devastating for *these* three to be resigned to their fates—kids with incredible strengths and powers who had no reason in the world to doubt themselves!

"Listen," she told them. "The feeling you're experiencing—as real as it might feel, it's *not.* He wants you to feel hopeless so you won't use your powers. And you're all *so* powerful. Aiko, you can move things with your mind alone. Lumierna, your metal-bending is legendary, and, Aristaeus—"

"I can harness the wind and the bees," he said dully. "Whoop-dee-doo. Having me here is the true mystery."

"I tried talking to them, too, when I first got here. Zumius told the guards to gag me," Augustus said softly.

"Me too," said Sakina.

"Well, we have to do *something*!" Diana said, frustration rising within her. They had the power to fight but not the will. "We need to turn this machine off."

"Keys?" Imani asked. "There's gotta be keys somewhere here."

"The guards have them," Sakina said. "They wear them on their belt, and they don't ever let them out of their sight."

"Diana"—Augustus eyed the door—"the guards could be back any second. They don't come on any schedule, but they're a bit overdue at this point. And with the window broken, they're going to know something is up right away."

Augustus was right. They had to act fast. Once the guards were here, if the kids weren't freed, it would be too late.

Diana looked at the machine. A keypad rested atop the narrowest end. She grabbed at it, but it was firmly embedded into the machine.

"Could this thing turn the machine off?" she asked.

"It's got a keypad to input a password," Imani said, examining it. "And a fingerprint recognition space. There's no way you'll be able to get in. Not in time."

Heavy footsteps sounded from outside. Diana's heart sank.

"Guards are coming!" Sakina said urgently. "You have to hide!"

Diana heard the jangling of keys on the other side of the door. Then a click as one of the locks began to turn.

They were here. Soon they'd be inside.

Diana breathed heavily as another lock turned. How many people would be on the other side? She'd spun in complete darkness to the land of the Targuni. She'd nearly lost her fingers and toes to frostbite on Targs. She'd fought a guard and broken out of Zumius's enclosure. She'd done so much. She'd fought so hard. She hadn't made it this far to lose now.

Chapter Twenty-Four

"Augustus, Sakina," Diana said urgently, "go back to where you were and pretend you're still tied up. They can't know you're free. We have to have the element of surprise on our side!" She turned to Imani. "You and I will blend into the wall," Diana said. "We'll stay hidden until they leave. Maybe in the meantime we'll figure something out."

Diana and Imani hurried to the far end of the room. Holding hands, they pressed their backs against the wall. The throbbing sensation passed over Diana as the door parted open. Two broad-shouldered men stepped inside.

"I'm telling you, Ronald," a mustachioed man told

the other, "you've got to try their fries one of these days. The honey mustard is unbeatable."

"I'll stick to my calzone, thanks," Ronald retorted. Then his voice grew quieter. "Hey, is there a fan on in here?"

"What're you talking about? There's no fan. Though there *should* be. The disinfectants are way too intense."

Both men's gazes shifted to the shattered window. The jagged edges. The shards strewn across the slick floor. The rain had eased, but wind still blew into the room.

Warily, they surveyed the area. "What happened?" the man with the mustache said shakily. "We were only gone twenty or thirty minutes."

"Don't know . . . but we should call for backup," Ronald said.

"You crazy?" The other man wiped his brow. "We weren't supposed to take a break at the same time. The boss will have our heads. Literally."

"It was your idea!" Ronald's eyes narrowed. "You said, 'There's seven locks. Nothing's gonna happen.' "

"Well, no time to play the blame game now!" the other man snarled. He marched behind the bookshelf to Augustus and Sakina.

"What happened?" he asked them.

"What do you mean?" Sakina said innocently, her arms perfectly hidden behind her body.

"Now, I *know* you had something to do with it." Ronald glared at her. "Your gag is off, and a skyscraper window is broken. We both know that doesn't happen all on its own."

"There's a shelf blocking our way," Augustus pointed out. "W-we indeed heard the loud noise, but we didn't see what happened."

"It was raining really hard. Thundering, too," Sakina said coolly. "Maybe a tiny tornado made its way over."

"Tiny tornado, huh?" He flashed her an annoyed look. "You think this is funny?"

"A little bit." Sakina shrugged.

"Sounds to me like you had something to do with it," he said. "You know both of you are completely expendable, right? He said so himself."

Sakina glared defiantly at the guard, but Diana saw how her lips trembled.

The guard moved toward her. He lifted the large brown nightstick over his head.

"You'll answer me one way or another." He leaned back. "I won't ask twice."

"Don't you dare!" Diana warned from her concealed location.

"What are you doing?" Imani gasped at her.

"Where'd that come from?" The men leapt back.

"Don't know . . ." Ronald eyed the children in their glass containers. "Can't be them. Too angry to be them."

"Maybe the solution is running low." The other guard moved toward the machine. "I'll turn the dial up a notch or three."

"The boss said he's the only one to do that."

"Yeah, well, he left *us* in charge, didn't he?"

Diana's eyes widened. The kids were already completely lethargic as it was! What would turning up the dial do to them? She could not let them do it. Releasing Imani's hand, she stepped away from the wall. She could feel Imani's incredulous eyes upon her. But she had to stop the guards from causing more harm than they already had.

"Do not touch the dial," she said evenly, her hands clenched into fists at her sides.

The guards' frowns shifted to surprise. They gaped at Diana as though witnessing a ghost.

"Where did *you* come from?" the mustachioed guard asked. He turned to the window and stared at her. "No way . . ."

"Isn't that her?" Ronald said slowly. "The girl the boss is always going on and on about?"

"You mean Diana, princess of the Amazons?" she said evenly. "You bet."

They grew completely silent. One of them cleared his throat.

"They've been searching for you for hours. Thirty different guards, scouring the city." Ronald looked at the shattered window and back at her, slack-jawed. "Did you climb *up the building*?"

"Looks like it," Diana said. "Word of warning. You really don't want to tangle yourself up with me. Let these kids go. And if you do, I won't harm you."

The men glanced at each other.

"Look, miss," Ronald said. His voice shook. "W-we don't know what your powers are. We don't want any trouble. We're only following orders."

There it was again. *Following orders.* As though committing heinous acts of evil were justified because someone else asked you to do it. Did they honestly think that meant it didn't count?

"You don't have to follow orders. You have a choice," Diana replied. "Let these kids go. And nothing happens to you."

"Sorry, but Ronald's right." The other cleared his throat. "I don't know how you broke a window on a skyscraper, but we have to take you in."

In unison the two of them gingerly walked toward her. Diana drew her sword and held it at her side. They were tall and broad shouldered. And clearly afraid of whatever superpowers they thought she had. She had this to her advantage. Diana waited until they grew closer, and then, she ducked and sideswiped them, racing to the other end of the room.

"Hey!" Ronald broke into a run after her. Diana crouched, waiting for him to approach. He was almost there. His hands inches from her wrist. She sliced the air with her sword; it skimmed his arm.

"Ow!" He jumped back with a howl, cradling his arm.

The other one went for her. He raised his nightstick. Diana spun out of the way, and his blow struck the air so wildly he lost his balance and fell backward.

"This can end any time," Diana said evenly. "Unlock the kids. Let them go."

"Like . . . we . . . said . . ." Ronald breathed out. His face was as red as a ripe tomato. "We . . . can't . . . do . . . that."

Simultaneously, from opposite corners of the room, they ran toward her. Sakina and Augustus moved as though to run toward her, but Diana shook her head frantically. These guards needed to focus on Diana so she could dispatch them once and for all. She braced as they charged at her. As soon as they were close enough, she dropped to the floor and rolled effortlessly away. Both men slammed full force into one another.

"What . . . the . . . ," one of the men croaked out.

Both men's eyes glazed over. They slumped to the floor. Their eyes closed. Diana exhaled. They were knocked out. Maybe for only a few seconds, but a moment was all she needed. She whipped out the rope Sakina and Augustus had been tied in and bound each guard.

"Hey!" Ronald said groggily as he came to. "What gives?"

The other guard grunted awake. But it was too late. Their hands were tied behind their backs. Their expressions tensed as they pushed and pressed against their bindings.

Diana exhaled. Surely there was a key in one of their pockets—that was what Augustus had said, hadn't he? She needed to fish one out and open these cages.

A buzzing sound filled the air. Diana froze. A burst of warmth blew into the room and a shot of light poured into the area and overtook the space before her. The light grew blurry, shifting and shimmering until it grew sharper and crisper, coming clearer into focus. A man. Taller now in this room with its higher ceilings, but it was still him: Zumius. His hologram towered over Diana.

"Now, I think you've toyed enough with my guards," he said. "Don't you?"

Diana's hands trembled. She gripped her sword tighter. The projection before her wasn't real. It was a hologram. But he *was* real. He was somewhere. Was he in this very building they were in? She might have subdued the guards, but how in the world could she take on an illusion and win?

Chapter Twenty-Five

Zumius's eyes narrowed behind the mask.

"While I'm glad you showed up on your own accord, I am *not* pleased with the destruction of my window, nor am I exactly thrilled you decided to play hero at a kiddie playground. What was *that* about? The video is everywhere. Like I don't have enough on my plate! Quite the narcissist, aren't you?"

What are you? Diana wondered. To have taken down kids with superpowers, and trapped them with glass and hopelessness, he had to be a sorcerer of some sort.

"I suggest you go ahead and get in the glass box yourself," he said. "Wouldn't you agree, children? It's futile to fight."

"Futile," the captured kids said at the same time.

"I'll get her eventually, won't I?"

"You will," Lumierna said dully.

"We can do this the easy way, or the hard way," Zumius said. "But the facts are the facts. This is my building. I own it. It's filled with my people. You are outnumbered. I'd say giving up would be the wise and rational thing to do."

If he thought she'd give up, he clearly knew *nothing* about her. Her mind raced. This was a hologram, but his hold on the guards in this building remained all too real. *Where are you?* Diana fumed. *Where are you, really?* She scanned the room. Was he projecting himself from inside this very building? She looked at the windows. The white walls. The bookshelf. High on the back wall, next to the metal door, she spotted a mirror encased in gold. It was as large as she was. Diana frowned. She'd seen a mirror identical to this one before. It was atop the fireplace in the home she'd found herself in when she first arrived in the mortal world. It couldn't be a coincidence. Maybe it was where the hologram was projecting from, thought

Diana. Did this mean the *actual* Zumius was behind it?

"Sounds like you want to do it the difficult way." His voice had a harder edge to it.

"I can grab her, sir," a guard shouted from outside the door.

"No," he said. "Eliot can handle this."

"Eliot?" the guard said, startled. "You sure, sir? After what happened?"

"Well, he's the only one besides myself with the training on Netta; I paid a hefty sum for it last week, not a moment too soon."

Footsteps echoed. She knew the man who entered. It was the guard she'd seen before, in the home with the cage. The one she'd locked up. Who'd begged her not to kill him. He held an enormous black device in his hand. She had no idea what it did, but she knew she did not want to find out.

"All right," Zumius said with a smile. "Eliot, Diana has gotten the better of beings with twice your capabilities, so I'm willing to let her getting the better of you slide, but it is time to redeem yourself after the complete bungling earlier today."

Eliot looked down at the contraption in his hand. Diana's heart raced. In a few seconds, he'd deploy it. Whatever it was, she wanted to make sure she didn't get tangled up in it.

The keys. Diana looked at the bound men on the floor. They had a key to the cages. If she could get them, she could work on getting at least one of the kids out. One would be enough to help her. So long as breaking them free of the machine broke them from their desolation. Before she could do anything, a voice cried out.

"Leave her alone!" Imani shouted.

"Where did that come from?" Zumius demanded. The holographic image whipped its head back and forth.

No. No. Diana frantically shook her head. *Imani! You can't come out. It's not real.*

Before her eyes, Imani emerged from her hiding spot. She charged toward Zumius, her hands clenched into fists. Diana winced as Imani tried to land a blow and tumbled straight through him instead. Her side hit the edge of an empty glass cage. She winced in pain. Gasping, she looked up, horrified.

"Run!" Diana screamed. "Blend! Hurry!"

Before Imani could do anything, two new guards stormed into the room. One yanked her by the arm, the other roughly by her wrist.

"Let me go!" she screamed. Diana moved toward her, but it was too late. Within half a second, they'd deposited her in the restraints. Magnets and wires were hastily taped to her arms.

"You're not going to win!" Imani shouted. Her face was flushed as she strained against the restraints. "You're not . . ." Her voice faded. Then her eyes shifted and she grew silent.

"See?" Lumierna said dully. "Told ya."

Tears filled Diana's eyes. After everything she and the girl from the mortal world had been through together, these guards had gotten Imani. The guards turned toward Diana. Diana eyed them carefully. She *had* to get their keys. But, glancing sideways at Eliot, she saw that he was still there, holding the weapon. Would he use it if she tried to retrieve them? Diana looked up at the mirror. He was up there. Zumius. She had no proof of it—but the feeling grew more and more certain in her gut.

"Eliot, get on with it," Zumius said. "Show me you're made of tougher mettle than you've demonstrated."

Eliot stood frozen at the edge of the room, and his mouth parted slightly at the sight of the children in glass. Was he hesitating? Had Diana's words to him earlier made him realize his mistake? She waited, tense. Whatever he had in his hand was something Zumius was counting on to subdue her. She had to see what was behind the mirror before he did.

"What are you waiting for?" asked Zumius. "Get her!"

"I'll get her!" the other guards who'd captured Imani cried out simultaneously. "Two of us can take her on."

They marched toward her. Diana grabbed her lasso and swung it toward them. Both men dropped to the floor. Their nightsticks fell. Diana smiled. *There we go.* In an instant, she wound the lasso around a nightstick. The guards' expressions paled as she pulled it to herself. They braced themselves. Waiting for her to launch it at them. Diana hefted it up with one hand and clutched it tightly. She turned toward the mirror and leaned back.

"No!" Zumius's voice thundered, vibrating in the room. "Don't you dare."

There *was* something behind the glass mirror. Gritting her jaw, she flung the instrument like a baton. It torpedoed toward the glass, circling rapidly before it slammed into it with a shattering crunch. The glass crumpled. Like a waterfall, it tumbled to the floor in shards. Diana watched with bated breath. Zumius's hologram began to shimmer, glitching in and out of view. Then it vanished. Behind what had once been the glass mirror was a room, warmly lit. Along one wall were beeping lights and metal levers . . . and a man, slender and scarcely taller than Diana. He stood in the center of the broken frame. Glass shards coated his masked face. Yanking off his disguise, he shook off the debris. Diana gaped at him. He had shoulder-length hair the color of straw. He wore wire-rimmed glasses with thick lenses. Sparse hair grew from his chin.

This was Zumius?

Chapter Twenty-Six

For a long moment, no one spoke. Everyone stared in stunned silence. Diana's mind raced. She took in his slumped shoulders and mealy-mouthed expression. After all she had been through in this past week, was *this* the man who had tried to destroy her home? Who had paid to kidnap children? Who had tormented the gods?

"Wait . . . ," one of the new guards said. "Are *you* Zumius?"

"Hey, I know you . . . ," the other said, a flicker of recognition crossing his face. "Kenneth Brown. You interviewed me for the gig. You said you were the manager. . . ."

"Yeah!" Eliot stared at him. "We always chat in

line at the coffee shop. You get the weird little vanilla-and-peppermint combo."

The man's ears turned bright pink. He crossed his arms.

"Careful how you speak to me. Regardless of what I actually look like, or what I drink, I am still your boss."

"Sorry, Kenneth. I mean, Mr. Brown," the guard said nervously.

"Zumius!" the man bellowed. "My name is Zumius!"

Diana felt as if the entire room were shifting beneath her feet. She knew that the person who'd hovered in front of her had been a projection. But from what she now gathered—the way the guards knew him, how he'd successfully played himself off as the building manager—this was a mortal. A human, and unexceptional to boot! She had never imagined that the person who had haunted the gods and had so severely affected their powers and tormented her beyond the ends of the earth was someone *from* the mortal world.

"So." One of the guards scratched his head. "You

don't have any magic abilities or nothing like that? You're just like us?"

"I am *nothing* like any of you," he snarled. "And if you don't comply, you will be sorry."

"Your guards don't look so sure anymore, Kenneth," Diana said evenly.

The man's nostrils flared. "Our names are what our parents give us. We get no say in the matter, do we? Zumius is the name I chose for myself. It's the person I am. Who I decided to be."

"And you decided to be *this*?" Diana's voice rose. "A vile person who would stop at nothing to tear families and worlds apart?"

"I'm beginning to think Hades was right," he said. "You really might be more trouble than you are worth."

"*How* could you do this? You're a mortal!"

"What, it's not possible for a mortal to best the gods and all you hold dear?" He beamed. "This is ultimately the problem with your people—your sheer arrogance. No one can touch you, that's what you all think. It's how I worked so long without anyone suspecting a thing. I've researched your world since I was a teenager. I knew those Greek stories weren't actually myths—it's what they wanted us to think. And when my parents left me their substantial inheritance, I used it wisely, to develop the Splectra. It took a few trials and errors, but now all is in place. And tonight? It will finally be time. This machine will combine your collective powers and make them mine, and I will be more powerful than anyone who's ever existed or will ever exist—and I can't *wait* to round up the gods and show them exactly who's boss now. Soon enough, the world, the galaxies, will all belong to me!"

Diana swallowed. How unexpected this evil turned out to be. A mortal man with no abilities to speak of turning the worlds upside down. He wanted to use everyone here—*including herself!*—in pursuit of evil. He had no power to speak of for himself—*that* was why he needed the children to accomplish his plans for him.

"How many times must I ask, Eliot?" Zumius shouted at the guard standing at the edge once more. "She won't trap herself."

Eliot glanced at Zumius. "I—I don't get it," he

said. "Why didn't you say so? Why'd you have to put on a mask and do the whole projection bit?"

"This isn't the time for chitchat," the man hissed. "Do what you have been compensated amply to do, or pay the price."

Eliot looked at Diana. Then he leaned down and placed the weapon on the floor. Rising up, he folded his arms.

"You will be sorry for that. *Very* sorry," Zumius said. Turning to the other guards, he barked, "Well, *one* of you get her. Do it quickly and I'll double your month's earnings."

This seemed to do the trick. Hesitating, one of the guards tentatively moved toward her. Diana examined the shattered space where Zumius stood. The opening was ten feet high, practically an entire story above her. If she could get herself up there, she could rope him in. She could take him down. There was a hanging light inside the room—if she lassoed her rope around it, she could use it to propel herself right into the room. If she did it quickly enough, he wouldn't even have a chance to yank the rope off before she leapt inside. The rope wasn't long enough to reach the light from where she stood, but—Diana glanced at the machine—if she climbed onto that thing, she could do it.

The guard was mere feet away from Diana. In one leap, she hopped atop the machine. She swung her lasso, readying to fling it at the lamp. She'd need to be quick. It was the only way.

"I wouldn't do that if I were you," Zumius warned. "Not unless you want to say goodbye to Sakina and Augustus."

Diana froze.

"Luca. Daniel!" he said. "It's time. Go to the expendables."

"What are you doing?" she began. But then, she paused. From her spot atop the machine she could see over the bookshelf. The men stood beside both Augustus and Sakina. Sharp daggers were aimed toward the children.

"Don't you dare," Diana said in a low voice.

"These two were fun surprises on my quest for *you*." Zumius shrugged. "I like to think of them as bonus kids since they are not in any way critical to my mission, but, hey, who wouldn't want an animal translator and a gifted potion maker on their team? However, they were brought here more so to be my fail-safe for a moment exactly like this. To bring *you* in line."

"What do you want?"

"It's really not complicated. Get off my extremely expensive machine. Stop with this futile fighting. And get in line. Now, tell me you understand. Those are the only words I want to hear. Anything else, even one move in any direction, and both of your friends die. It's as simple as that. And you alone will bear the responsibility for it."

"No!" Sakina shouted. "Don't listen to him! Get him, Diana! You're so close!"

"Sakina's right," Augustus said in a trembling voice. "Y-you're this close to saving all of humanity. G-get him. Don't stop because of us."

"Silence!" Zumius shouted.

Diana's chest tightened. She *was* so close. Zumius was *right there.* But glancing at her friends, she felt a tear slip down her cheek. If there was even a chance he'd follow through on his threat. . . . She could never allow it to happen.

"I understand." She dropped her hands to her sides in surrender.

Chapter Twenty-Seven

"Ever heard of the word kismet, Diana?" Zumius said from his perch.

Diana stiffly let a new guard lead her to the machine.

"It's of Arabic origin, did you know? No—of course you didn't." He sneered. "It's what happens when the stars align and everything goes peachy, exactly like it was meant to. And today, this is basically what happened. I guess I have you to thank for unveiling who I truly am." He laughed. "I've kept it hidden so long. Thought a costume would be more on brand, but I think the truth really does set you free."

The guard shoved her into the glass container.

She heard Sakina's silent sobs and pushed down her own tears as the guard stuck a magnet onto her skin. Restraints looped over her arms. With a sense of finality, the glass door closed. A lock clicked.

"What is this thing?" she asked shakily. "What do these wires do?"

"This *thing*?" He frowned. "Manners, Diana! This 'thing' is only the finest contraption ever created," he said. "And you'll find out soon enough what those wires do. Maybe then you'll develop a bit of respect for my intellectual superiority."

"You're not intellectually superior," Diana said. "Just born into wealth. And evil enough to want to harm as many people as you can."

His nostrils flared.

"Only someone with a pea-sized brain wouldn't see how superior I am to you. In every way." Spittle flew from his mouth. "And in a few hours, I will own your abilities."

Before Diana could respond, he slipped out of view. Moments later, he reappeared. This time, through the metal door. He walked toward her until he was only inches away. It was hard to wrap her mind around how evil could take on the cover of such ordinariness. He picked up a vial from the shelf and showed it to her proudly.

"See?" he said. "A sip of this and I get to harness your abilities, but this method is not ideal as I can only possess your powers for as long as the liquid remains in my system. But once I have all your powers inputted into the Splectra at the exact moment of alignment, it will mix up together nicely and transfer your powers to me permanently. I won't need stinky vials anymore. And come to think of it"—his lips curled into a smile—"I suppose I won't need any of *you,* either."

"You'll never win," she countered. She felt no hopelessness yet—only revulsion and anger.

"You're not the sharpest tool in the shed, now, are you?" He laughed. "Don't you see? I *have won.* Now, I've gotta know what all the fuss is with you. Better be worth it."

He walked up to the keypad at the narrow end of the device. After tapping it a few times, he pressed down forcefully. A beeping sound echoed in the room. The wires blinked red and yellow.

"Ouch!" Diana cried out. Intense heat pressed against her arm.

A sliver of uncertainty suddenly crept over her. She pushed against her bindings. It couldn't be happening! But it was: doubt began to snake through Diana's body.

Zumius clapped his hands with delight.

"It's fun to see the most stubborn person face the inevitable," he said. "You are exactly why I had a turbo force feature. Glad it's working, because the truth is, your defeat *is* inevitable—may as well get used to it now. Ooh, now to explore your powers." He grinned widely. "This feels like Christmas!"

He unlocked a box that was set in the center of the machine. A green button jutted out. Before he could press it, a guard raced inside.

"A problem!" he panted. "A major problem. We gotta alert the boss."

"What is it?" He scowled. "Can't you see I'm busy?"

"I was looking for Zumius . . ." The guard eyed Zumius warily. "I need to speak to him immediately."

"You're speaking to him." He stomped a foot. "Get on with it."

The guard hesitated and looked at the others. They subtly nodded. One of them shrugged.

"Oh, my apologies." He cleared this throat. "I wanted to alert you that there are some police officers downstairs looking for you."

"So? Send them away," Zumius retorted. His hand hovered over the button.

"Uh, well." He shifted. "It's not so simple. There are two police cars and four officers downstairs. They got a phone call about someone scaling this building. They wanted to come in and inspect for themselves, and I was holding them off, but then they got to questioning us about why there are armed guards outside the building. Do we have a permit for that? I did my best to hold them off, but they're getting pushy."

"Thanks a lot, Diana," Zumius huffed. "Adding more work for me to do."

Diana fought against her draining emotions as best she could and shot him a look of hatred.

Zumius grudgingly moved away from the machine. "You all, come with me. Except you, Eliot." He glared at him. "You've proven yourself exceptionally useless. Stand guard outside the door. You can manage *this,* can't you?"

Everyone exited the room. Locks clicked shut. It was empty once more. Augustus and Sakina immediately raced over to Diana.

"We'll get you out of here," Augustus said.

They pulled and pushed against the door, but Diana knew their efforts would have no effect.

"Potions?" Diana managed to say. The resignation she felt swirled warm and syrupy, enticing her to surrender and let go. But she pushed against it. She wouldn't let it plant itself inside her. *It's not real. It's not real,* she kept telling herself. "Is there anything in there that could have any effect on this machine?"

"Nothing I can think of off the top of my head," Augustus said nervously. "B-but I'll try to come up with something."

"Sakina," Diana said. But before she could say more, an overwhelming wave of sadness passed over her. Sweat trickled down her brow. She wasn't afraid. She'd been afraid since this whole situation began at the Charà festival. This feeling—of surrender—it was far worse than any fear she had felt. Hopelessness squeezed her insides.

"Welcome to our world," Aiko said. "Looks like it's begun taking its effect on you, too."

"This feeling," Diana breathed out. "It's—it's brutal."

"Yep," Lumierna said. "But you kind of get used to it after a while. Sink into it. It makes it easier. The more you fight, the harder it pushes you down."

The wires were positioned in the center of her arm. She leaned her head down. She strained to reach them. If she could yank them out with her teeth. But what was the point? It wouldn't work, would it? Lumierna was right. The more she fought against her situation, the more discouraging thoughts filled her mind. It felt far easier to sink into the slow, easy sweetness of surrender. She was going to lose anyway, wasn't she? The gods were doomed. She had run away from home with the hopes of defeating this person, but how could she have had a chance to save anyone when she couldn't even get herself out of this?

"Diana," Sakina said in a panicked voice. "Push away the hopelessness! You can fight it! Think of your mom. The warrior women whose strength runs through your veins. Everyone who needs you. Channel it, Diana. You've done it before."

"I can't," Diana whispered. "I'm too tired."

"Come on, everyone," Sakina urged the others. "If all of you together fight this, it can work out. You've got to do it. You've got to at least give it everything you have!"

"Says the girl who is *not* hooked up," Aristaeus retorted.

"No use," Aiko said. "You don't get it. He'll win."

In the background, Diana could hear Augustus desperately digging through his bag.

"No. Not this one," he murmured. "Not this one, either . . ."

"But the feeling that this is unwinnable isn't the truth," Sakina said urgently. "You *can* beat him. It's a fact. It's like Diana said earlier. You all are probably the most powerful people in the mortal world, all gathered in one spot. Together you can take him down."

"Or maybe it's reality," one of them said. "The sooner we accept it, the less it all hurts."

Diana knew Sakina meant well. But the machine was too clever. It had locked the children in, not by a powerful weapon but by their own feelings. And at this moment these feelings were controlling the destiny of the entire world.

Augustus frantically opened and sniffed different potions.

"I'll find one," he said. "There's got to be something. We're not going to lose hope. We can do it."

Past Diana would have appreciated his reassurances, but to this Diana, the odds seemed insurmountable. She felt too resigned to hope.

Chapter Twenty-Eight

"I got it!" Augustus finally exclaimed.

"Something to break them out?" Sakina asked.

"Not exactly—but kind of," he said. "I think I've got the ingredients to make a universal antidote. It fights back whatever is in one's system. It doesn't work on *everything*, but it can help with lots of different charms. I don't have much on me. Barely enough for one person, but it could dull the effect at least for a little while. And I see some ingredients for another potion, too—it creates a memory fog. . . ."

"Just one thing at a time. We need the antidote!" Sakina urged.

Diana saw Augustus slip different ingredients,

both liquid and powder, into a glass vial. Carefully, he mixed it up. Sakina hurried toward Diana. She dragged a chair behind her. Hopping up, she turned to Augustus.

"Get it to me! I'll try to have her drink it. I should be able to reach the opening at the top of the enclosure with this chair!"

Augustus handed Sakina the antidote. With trembling hands, Sakina strained against the glass and leaned over the top of the enclosure, where the wire protruded from the glass cage.

"Open up," she said.

Diana looked up at Sakina. Her skin felt clammy. What if the potion didn't work? What if she ended up having a reaction? Was it worth it to even try? Really? Wouldn't the guards simply punish Sakina even more if they caught her in the act? If the liquid *did* work, maybe it would be better to give it to one of the other kids. Not her. She wasn't strong like Lumierna or able to harness the wind like Aristaeus. She didn't have any powers.

"Come on," Sakina urged gently. "Fight it, Diana. You can do it."

With trembling lips, Diana pushed away the thoughts swirling within her. She parted her lips. A sweet and slightly acidic liquid entered her mouth. It wet her tongue. She felt Augustus and Sakina watching her. It wouldn't work. Diana knew this. Nothing could stop this feeling. But then, like the tides of the ocean, she felt it. Bit by bit, her hopelessness was receding.

"It's working," Diana breathed out.

"Good," Sakina said. "Now let's work on getting you out of that. You can do it."

Diana struggled against her restraints. She pushed her legs against the straps tying her feet to the enclosure. She gritted her teeth and yanked her arms to loosen the bonds. But nothing worked. She was stuck.

"Can you make more for the other kids?" she asked Augustus. "I don't know how they've restrained us. I can't break out of it. But if all of us lost our despair . . . maybe we could do it. There's no way this machine could contain all of us if we were collectively ready to break out."

"I wish I could," Augustus said sadly. "But I barely

had enough for you. I have some memory fog, but I'm not sure how potent it is. It's very old."

"Sleep potion?" Diana said quickly. "Could we get some sleeping charm whipped up to throw on the guards when they come in? Something to put them all into an eternal sleep."

"I could check," he replied. He dug hurriedly through his bag. After a moment he paused. "The good news is, I have some of it," he said. "Enough for a few guards. But I don't have the key ingredient to make the sleep eternal."

"Could it put them to sleep for a little while?"

"Maybe," he said. "But who knows how long it'd last. Could be ten years. Could be ten minutes. Seconds. It'll be completely unpredictable."

"Better than nothing," Diana said. "Even three minutes gives us something to work with. And, Sakina, can you find some kind of a hook or something to yank these wires off me?"

"But I heard them say it could have disastrous side effects," Sakina said, hesitating.

"I think that was the hopelessness speaking,"

Diana said. "Let's take a risk on me. Let's see if it'll work!"

Sakina hurriedly searched the room for a way to disentangle the wire.

"Okay," Augustus said breathlessly. "It's almost ready!"

She watched Augustus stir the potion. Sakina searched frantically for some sort of hook or tool to pull out her wires as footsteps sounded in the distance. Augustus sifted powder and edged it into the glass bottle. Sparks fell on either side of the floor. The door's locks began to unclick. Though his hands trembled, Augustus did not run or hide. He grabbed the vial, hurried to the door, and waited. Eliot would be inside any second now.

But when the doors opened, Eliot didn't enter. Instead it was two other guards she'd seen before.

"I'm telling you, he can talk to the cops all he wants and make them get a warrant, but they'll be back," the guard named Daniel said. "Three different security guards from nearby buildings got video footage of the two of them climbing.

He can't chalk it up to a hoax. Any minute now a news team'll be here with helicopters and everything."

"How do you climb a skyscraper, though?" Luca scratched his head. "In the *rain*?"

"Dunno," Daniel said. He lowered his voice. "But if you ask me, now that we know what's behind the curtain, I'm starting to wonder if we're backing the wrong horse. That's gotta be what Eliot's thinking—acting as squirrelly as he is."

"Whoever Zumius really is, he's managed to accomplish a lot. I think he'll win," Luca said. "And we'll be his loyal guards who deserve the praise and the money that goes along with making him the most powerful man in the world."

Diana watched Augustus inch out of his hiding spot. The guards were so busy chatting, they didn't notice him easing up on them.

"Missing a kid?" Augustus asked. The guards startled. Before they could move, Augustus raised his arm and splashed the liquid onto them.

"How'd you break out?" Luca wiped the liquid from his nose and yanked Augustus by the wrist, drawing the boy toward him. Augustus crumpled like a paper doll under the tight grip. "They don't pay me enough for this," he growled.

"Tell Zumius he broke out," Daniel said, and shrugged. "I'll back you up. You did what you needed to do to defend your—"

Both men's eyes glazed over. Luca released Augustus's wrist. Within seconds, both men were sprawled on the floor, snoring. It had worked! Sakina raced over and dug through their vests, hurrying to find the keys.

"Did they really put those guards to sleep?" Aiko said slowly.

"Looks like it," Lumierna said.

Diana watched the other kids nervously.

"I think . . . I think. Maybe we should try," Aristaeus said. "If he could overtake those two, maybe we can do something if we all work together. What do you think?"

"I don't know," Imani said. "He'll get us again. It'll be worse then."

"If we try, we might get caught," Diana told them. "But *maybe* we'll take him down once and for all."

"Let's give it a whirl," Aiko said. "Let's try to break out together."

The fivesome closed their eyes. Their cheeks flushed from the effort. A popping sound burst in the air.

"I broke out of the arm restraint," Aiko said. "I—I did it."

"Me too," Lumierna said, startled.

Just then, the door parted—but this time it wasn't a guard. It was Zumius.

Chapter Twenty-Nine

Zumius strolled into the room. Glancing at the children, he took in their broken restraints. He jumped back, his eyes widened in horror.

"That's right," Aiko said triumphantly. "You underestimated us, and we're going to get out now. And you'll be sorry you messed with me. My mind-bending is going to—"

Before she could finish her sentence, Zumius sprinted toward the box and slammed the green button. Aiko's eyes grew distant. Diana gasped. Hopelessness rose within her. The air grew cold.

"Alfred!" Zumius thundered. "Get in here. Now!"

A guard raced into the room. He stepped over the unconscious guards and wordlessly grabbed

Augustus and Sakina. With new rope, he yanked them to the wall and tied them to their post.

"I can't feel my hands!" Sakina cried out.

"Good!" Zumius snapped. "It's what you deserve."

"The police, sir," the guard said. "If they manage to come back sooner than later . . . should we move the children?"

"Move them?" He snorted. "Why? It's already over. The alignment's gonna start any minute now, and when it does, no piece of paper they trot out will mean a thing."

"Still," the guard said nervously. "Just in case?"

"All right." Zumius scowled. "Tell the guards up front to make sure the helicopter is ready if we need it."

Zumius opened a compartment in the machine. He held up a wired magnet, much like the ones attached to the children. He smirked at Diana.

"The time has come, Diana. Now I'll find out what your powers—or should I say *my* soon-to-be-powers—are, once and for all."

"You . . . won't . . . win . . . ," Diana managed to say.

"Cute that you're still trying to push back," he said, and chuckled. "Now, while we wait for the alignment, let's see what you've got cooking." He pressed a new button. The machine buzzed. The glass compartments the children were in began to tremble.

"Ah, now here we go!" Zumius exclaimed. "First, as usual, Aristaeus." Zumius's eyes were half-closed as though in meditation. "You've always been under-estimated, Ari. But never by me. *I've* never doubted how important your skills are."

Zumius clapped his hands. A burst of wind whipped through the broken window and swept into the room. Waving his arms like a conductor of an orchestra, Zumius rippled the wind along the ceiling. The air lifted Sakina and Augustus three feet in the air, their roped hands sliding along the metal handle. The wind lifted the sleeping guards from the floor, then slammed them down with a resounding thump.

"Being able to have the wind at your fingertips is a great skill. All I gotta do is snap my fingers, and

I can raise the waves of the ocean and spin tornadoes.

"Ah, and Lumierna." He leaned over to the shelf and picked up a pen. Pressing it between his hands, he crumpled it like paper. "Yours is more of a meat-and-potatoes kind of skill, but this makes it no less exciting to control. You must have the ability to meld one of the strongest elements in the universe if you are to rule it."

"And Aiko," he shouted, and cackled.

"Go . . . eat . . . a . . . bug," she panted.

"With your powers, I was able to mess with the gods," he retorted. "Able to taunt them from afar. Snag their powers with my mind. It was a delight. Truly."

"And now for you, Diana." He smiled viciously. "Let's see what you've got!"

"Whatever intelligence you received about me, it wasn't accurate," Diana said.

"Still trying to cover it up," he said. "I admire your commitment."

Diana felt something tingling against her arm. She shivered.

"Ah, there's your strength." He leaned his arm toward a nearby wall. With a jab, he punched a hole straight through the wall. "And, ooh, the speed!" His eyes brightened. He began to run in place, moving so fast that his legs soon became a blur.

Diana stared at him. What was happening?

"Ah! And these reflexes are a delight. . . . Eliot!" he called.

Eliot reluctantly peeked inside.

"Throw your nightstick at me!" Zumius shouted. "Straight at my head."

"Ah . . . the nightstick?" Eliot asked nervously. "You want me to throw it *at* you?"

"You heard me, didn't you?" His eyes narrowed. "Do it."

Eliot bit his lip. Then he flung the nightstick straight at Zumius. Milliseconds before it hit his head, Zumius lifted a hand and shoved it away. His arm had moved so quickly it blurred the air.

"And now, this one . . ." He grinned. "Flight."

Diana was about to argue when a gust of wind swept again into the room and encircled his body. To Diana's astonishment, Zumius was levitating; his feet rose off the floor. He swam up with his arms and shot upward until he tapped the top of the ten-foot ceiling. Diana felt lightheaded. This wasn't possible! She couldn't fly. She thought of how she'd fallen from the building—how she'd swum up to save herself and Imani. But that was Zeus . . . wasn't it?

"Oh, come on now. What is *this*?" He curled his mouth in distaste. "What is this feeling? This fuzzy sensation?" He studied the machine. "Love?" He guffawed. "That's not a superpower. I'd say it's more your Achilles' heel than anything else. After all, love brought you into my lab voluntarily. Love made you turn yourself in to protect your little friends when, let's be real, you could've destroyed me in an instant. I'd say love is as useless a power as any."

Salty tears ran down Diana's cheeks. It was over. She couldn't physically break free, and now she, along with these other children, would be responsible for harming the entire world—the *universe.* For destroying the reign of the gods. For destroying her home. She thought of Aunt Antiope with her brilliant smile. How she could always cheer Diana up. How she doted on her. Her mother, Queen

Hippolyta, was overprotective, but it was because she loved Diana so very much. More than anything in the world, she wanted Diana safe and happy.

Diana thought of her wolf companion, Binti. The Sky Kangas that indulged her with adventures through Themyscira. Cylinda and Yen, who, even though she was younger than them, never made her feel unwelcome. They always treated her like their peer. What would become of all of them? How would they fight this off?

A tinge of smoke rose from the machine. Zumius, so immersed in trying out his new powers, hadn't noticed.

She looked at her best friend, Sakina, struggling against her bindings. Augustus sobbed openly. Imani's eyes pressed closed. They were all at his mercy. So many people—those whom she knew, and all the innocents she did not know—would be irrevocably hurt by this man. Her heart felt like it was breaking. A real and physical break.

"Cheer up. There *is* a bright side," Zumius said as he continued to test his abilities. "No matter what happens to everyone else, you all will be safe, just in case I should ever need to re-download your powers. There is comfort in that."

"We will never work for you," Sakina said.

"You both are dispensable," he said with a glare. "Don't forget it."

"You will *not* hurt them," Diana growled. Sakina and Augustus had worked selflessly, risking their lives to help everyone—and how he taunted both of them now!

"Not only will I harm them if I choose to," Zumius retorted, "but *you* will help me do it." He moved to continue speaking, but as he turned to the machine, his eyebrows shot up. The machine was smoking, trembling. He raced to press a button, but before he could, he shrieked. The magnet attached to his arm was steaming. He yanked roughly at it.

"Owww!" he yelled. "It's stuck!"

Diana stared as smoke rose from Zumius's arm. The machine began to shake aggressively. But the timing . . . was it a natural malfunction? Was Zumius drawing too much power from it during the transfer? Come to think of it, the machine had only begun to act up once Diana started thinking of those she loved. . . .

Was it a coincidence? Or was love the one power the machine couldn't handle?

Diana focused now. She scrunched her forehead as she thought of Arya, Sakina's feline pet, and the women she'd met at the Charà festival. Their laughter and their kindness. She thought of Liara and her sweet brown dragon eyes and the way she had lovingly been Diana's companion on their journey together. She thought of Proteus, who had fed her when she was hungry, and the dolphin that had saved her life when she'd been lost and ready to give up at sea.

"Ahhh!" Zumius cried out. Steam rose from his arm. "Eliot! Why are you standing there? Do something!"

Eliot stared at the machine. Bursts of sparks flew out, landing on the floor around the glass enclosures. Diana felt her hopelessness drift away. The other children trapped alongside her blinked. Their stupor, too, seemed to be fading. Diana felt shaky. It was true—her love and thoughts of love affected the machine's powers! Maybe her love *was* a superpower. If it was, then it was a power that someone as evil as Zumius could never understand. And even if he could, it was a power he could never wield, because love would never aid Zumius in destroying the world. Diana gritted her teeth and kept focusing—she would wield her love to end this imprisonment once and for all.

"The machine is malfunctioning," Lumierna said.

"Yeah," Aiko said. "I . . . I feel more like myself."

"Me too," said Aristaeus.

"Eliot!" Zumius shouted.

"It's now or never!" Diana yelled. "On the count of three, we break out."

"You will do no such thing! Owwww!" Zumius screeched. He pulled at the wire, but it seemed melted onto him. He fell to the floor in agony.

"One . . . two . . . three—now!" Diana strained against her bindings along with the others. The machine smoked more and more, and it shook so hard the floor began to vibrate. A button popped off and flew toward the jagged open window.

"No!" Zumius groaned.

Lumierna and Diana wrenched off their restraints. They yanked off their wires. Aiko followed suit. Clenching their jaws, they pushed against the enclosure. A cracking sound filled the room. They were almost out. The glass was about to break. They were so close.

Zumius raced for the shelf but flinched. The magnet was still attached to his arm. He could only go so far. Straining, he inched his fingers toward a vial. Diana knew what he was trying to do. He was trying to grab one last vial of his special potion, to drink it and gain some of their powers and fight back.

Eliot walked toward Zumius. Only three of the children had broken off their restraints and the wires. Ari and Imani were still struggling. Would three of them be enough to take Zumius down if he drank one of those potions?

Eliot picked up the vial Zumius strained for.

"There we go," Zumius gasped. "Pour it straight into my mouth. Even a few drops will do the trick."

But instead of handing it to Zumius, Eliot tossed the vial onto the floor. It bounced against the marble surface once before smashing into pieces and spilling the liquid.

"What. Are. You. Doing?" Zumius stared at him, astonished.

"What I should have done long ago." Eliot looked at Diana. "I needed to get knocked into my senses by someone, I suppose."

"You imbecile!" Zumius shouted.

With a firm shove, Eliot pushed the bookshelf. It trembled before tipping backward and landing on the floor with a shuddering crash. All the vials shattered as they fell to the floor.

"I did it!" Lumierna exclaimed. The door to their enclosure popped out. Hurriedly, they raced to Imani and Ari, yanking off their doors as easily as flicking a pebble. Now everyone was free.

Zumius writhed and howled on the floor. He thrashed his arms and legs.

"Thank you," Diana said to Eliot.

"Had to make it up to you and everyone I harmed somehow," Eliot said. "Not that any of this will be close to making it right."

"It's more than you know," Diana said. "You helped save the world. I'd say that's a good place to start."

She looked at the machine, then at Zumius. They were free, but Zumius was still there. They had to do something about him once and for all.

Chapter Thirty

Lumierna, Aiko, Aristaeus, and Imani approached Zumius. Diana ran to Sakina and Augustus and untied them.

The man lay panting on the floor. The machine was no longer buzzing. All the lights were off. Smoke poured from all sides of the contraption. Yanking off his magnets, he looked up at the circle of children and shrank back.

"Look," he said, shakily, "we can work something out."

"Yeah?" Lumierna said, cocking their head.

"You're not thrilled with me. I get it. But hear me out! I'm rich. Super rich. We can find a solution to make us all happy. A win-win. Hey, how about a partnership? We could team up."

"Team up? With you?" Aiko raised an eyebrow.

Before anyone could reply, the metal door parted. Three guards hurried inside. They skidded to a stop upon seeing Zumius writhing on the floor.

"There they are!" Zumius cried. Spittle flew from his mouth. "Grab them!"

"What happened to teaming up?" Diana said, joining the others.

"What a shocker, he wasn't true to his word," Imani retorted. She looked at the guards. "If I were you, I'd drop those weapons."

"I'd listen to her," Aristaeus said. He raised a hand. A small whirlwind formed before their eyes outside the broken window—it hovered at the edge, spinning like a cyclone.

The guards stared at the tornado, then at the children, and quickly dropped their weapons and raised their palms in surrender.

"Great!" Lumierna looked at the machine. "Now,

for starters, I think we should do something about this hulk of metal here."

Lumierna walked toward the Splectra. This machine had tormented all the children for so long. Lumierna pressed their hands on the smooth exterior and gripped it with white knuckles. Beneath their touch it began to crinkle and crumple. Gripping one end, Lumierna drew it inward, toward themself, before folding the machine in half as easily as a blanket.

"My baby!" Zumius cried out. "Don't destroy my baby!" He scrambled to rise, but Aiko shot him a look and whipped her head to the side. Zumius shrank back.

Lumierna folded the machine more and more, crumpling it smaller and smaller, until it was a ball the size of their fist.

"Pretty sure that's taken care of," they said, tossing it down with finality.

Sakina raced over and hugged Diana.

"You did it. You all did it!" she cried.

Diana looked at the others—some of their eyes

filled with tears of relief. They just had to figure out what to do with Zumius, and then—

"Not. So. Fast."

Before she could move, Zumius lunged for the Netta device Eliot had laid on the floor and jabbed a button. A gossamer web sprang toward them.

"Run!" Diana screamed.

But it was too late—within a millisecond the web wrapped itself around them.

"Ha!" he wheezed. "Dear old Netta came through. My precious fail-safe."

"I got this," Lumierna said angrily. They grasped at the net, pulling at the fine fabric. But try as they might, they couldn't grasp it between their fingers.

"Th-there's nothing metal in this thing at all." Their expression paled. "And whatever material it is, I can't even grab on to any of it."

"I can't reach him through this thing, either!" Aiko grew flushed.

"Consider yourselves lucky, I guess. You'll get to live until I can rebuild my machine," Zumius said.

Augustus raced toward Zumius with a vial in his

hand. But as Augustus neared him, he tripped over his own feet. Diana winced as the vial flew into the air and landed on the floor with a crack. Whatever was in there was gone.

"Get him," Zumius ordered the guards. "And grab Eliot, the traitor, while you're at it."

As the guards marched toward Eliot and Augustus, a gray mist rose from where the bottle had shattered. The guards' gait slowed. They frowned.

"Wait—what are we supposed to do?" one of them asked.

"What do you mean, what are you supposed to do?" Zumius glared at them, but then his own expression grew more puzzled. "I told you . . . didn't I?"

"It's the memory fog spell!" Augustus shouted. "It won't last long—but they're distracted for now. You have maybe five minutes." He faltered. "I think?" The spell was clearly affecting him, too.

"I can help," Eliot said. He paused. "I think?"

Five minutes. To do what? Diana glanced about. Eliot might have helped them, but the charm had deployed on him as well. Sakina, too, looked bewildered. It seemed the net protected them from the effects of the charm, but how were they going to break out if Lumierna couldn't tear apart this fabric? If Aiko couldn't mind-bend? Imani couldn't help them here, either. She reached out and touched the edge of the fabric. It was silky, soft, and billowy . . .

She glanced at Aristaeus. Her eyes widened.

"The wind—" she said. "This material is tough to break out of, but what if we don't rip it apart—what if we flip it into the air?"

"Not following you." Aristaeus stared at her.

"You could harness the wind, and we could get this net to fly off us. You could do that, couldn't you?"

"But if Aiko's and Lumierna's powers don't work in here, how could mine?"

"He hasn't tied up the net." Diana pointed to the narrow opening at the end of the net—it was so small, barely the width of a needle. . . . "There's still space to summon the wind—not much—but maybe it would be enough?"

Aristaeus bit his lip. Then he looked at Diana. "Guess there's only one way to find out."

He lifted his hands and closed his eyes. Diana

held her breath—waiting. Would it work? And if it didn't . . . what would they do next?

But then—air poured into their space, billowed out the material, widening it until it was as though they stood inside a bubble.

"Hey—" Zumius began. His eyes were sharpening into focus.

Before he could do anything, Aristaeus lifted his hands and shouted: "Now!"

The net zipped into the air and flipped inside out—and in one swoop it scooped Zumius and the guards into its grasp.

"Noooooo!" Zumius shouted. He pounded against the material—but just as it had been for the kids, breaking out with sheer force proved impossible.

"We need to tie it up!" Diana shouted. "So they can't break out."

"I can help." Lumierna picked up a metal stool, and with their hands they twisted it like it was clay, until it was long and narrow. Swiftly, they used it to tie up the opening of the net.

"What do we do about him, though?" Imani said. "We can't leave him there, can we?"

"I could take care of *that,* too." Lumierna clenched their palms into fists. Zumius shrank back and whimpered.

"I don't want him killed," Diana said. "He should have to answer for what he's done. I want justice to be served. We deserve that."

"But what if he figures out a way to break out?" Imani asked worriedly.

"I can help with that." Aiko smiled.

"No! Wait!" Zumius shook his head. "Listen—"

Before he could finish his sentence, Aiko shot him a hard gaze. Zumius blinked. He shrank backward and curled into a ball. He opened and closed his mouth, but no words came out.

"Looks like you can't use your skills inside the net, but you can get through from the outside. That should do it." Aiko grinned. "He won't be trying to outtalk us anytime soon."

"So it's over?" Imani trembled. "It's really over?"

"We . . . we did it," Ari said slowly. He looked

down at Zumius, and then up at everyone, his eyes widening. "We really did it!"

Lumierna whooped and shouted. They high-fived everyone. Augustus and Sakina pulled Diana into a group hug. Soon everyone was hugging. Diana laughed as she looked at everyone's shining faces. They'd done it! They'd done what no one else—not even the gods themselves—had been able to do: they'd taken down Zumius! He was tied up, immobilized.

She felt herself go weak with relief. It was over. The nightmare that began just a week earlier when Augustus had shown up on Themyscira was finally behind them.

"So . . . what about him?" Ari asked, his hands on his hips.

"He can't hurt us anymore." Diana looked down at him. "The gods should get their powers back soon enough . . . they can deal with him."

"How do we get home?" Aiko asked.

"Portals," Aristaeus said. "That's how I was brought here. A cage reconfigured from a portal transported me."

"From what I heard, they only can transport those who are specified for transportation," Lumierna said.

"How do you specify?" Aristaeus asked. "Is there some magic word?"

"I . . . I don't know," Diana admitted.

"So now what?" Aiko asked, crestfallen. "Are we stuck in the mortal world forever?"

There was no way! Diana moved to comfort her—but what exactly *did* come next? They'd overtaken Zumius. He was no longer a threat—the gods *could* take care of him—but first the gods would need to find *them.*

"For now, come to my place," Imani said. "It's not far from here. You're welcome to stay as long as you need until you can figure things out."

"But there are armed guards at the entrance of the building. And I saw lasers in the front lobby. Who knows what else is waiting for us? Though I guess we *could* take them down in a fight," Diana said slowly. The joy from moments earlier deflated a little. Exhaustion ebbed through her body. Diana didn't know how much more fighting she could handle.

"I have a better idea." Aristaeus walked to the window and raised a hand. Wind blew through the window and swirled around them. Aristaeus drew his fingers to his lips and whistled. Within moments, a buzzing sound thundered outside. Diana flinched, half expecting the dragonfly creatures of Targs to fly in. Instead, thousands of bees filled the room.

"Uh . . ." Imani blinked. The buzzing sound filled the space.

"Don't worry!" Aristaeus called out over the din. "They're going to give us a ride to your place. Jump out the window, and the bees and the wind will do the work. I'll go first."

He stepped out the window and leapt into the air. Diana's breath caught in her throat. The bees propelled Aristaeus in the air. Diana shivered. They held him much like the Xerx of Targs had held Diana up not so long ago. But this time was different. These creatures promised safety. Imani tapped her hands against the bees and closed her eyes—and within seconds, they flew invisibly through the air.

As the kids let the bees sweep them up, Imani guided them to her home.

"Straight over this batch of trees. Then follow the asphalt highway," she said, craning her neck down to check. Buildings and lakes, rooftops and wooded forests swept below them. Diana felt a weightlessness as they undulated against the wind. But the sensation in her stomach was not only from the bees—it was from realizing they'd done it.

After all she had been through, they had won. Zumius was taken down. Now . . . they just had to figure out how to get back home.

Chapter Thirty-One

"My mom doesn't get off work until six o'clock in the morning," Imani said as they hurried inside her home. "But I'm sure once I explain everything, she won't mind hosting you all until you can figure out what to do next, though," she said, and shook her head. "Explaining it will be *interesting.*"

Once inside, Aristaeus flopped onto a sofa. A gust of wind fluttered the curtains. He leaned back and closed his eyes. "I could sleep for a thousand years."

"Me too." Aiko yawned.

Diana fidgeted. Imani was kind, and she *hoped* Imani's mother would understand. But all she wanted was to fall asleep in her own bed. After all they'd been through, exhaustion crept through her body along with a homesickness so deep and so real she ached.

"Mind if I make some tea?" Aiko asked. "I could use a boost."

"Help yourself," Imani said. "Third cabinet to the right."

Aiko pulled out a pot hanging above and filled it with water. A sweet, lemony ginger scent filled the home as a knock sounded on the front door.

"Uh-oh." Imani rose.

"Don't worry," Aiko said. "Whoever it is, we've got them."

"Diana!" a voice cried from the other side. "Imani! Open up. It's us!"

"Oh," Diana said. "The god squad."

The foursome opened the door and stumbled into the foyer.

"Diana! Imani! So glad you're okay!" Shaina swept both girls into her arms and hugged them tightly. "Thank the gods. You're *all* here."

"We planned to get to you once we fought the guards off," said Anand. "But the fight got out of hand. The police arrived, and it became a huge mess. We managed to get away, but we were pretty beaten up."

"Then, a little while ago, our wounds began to heal." Shaina smiled. "And we knew—you all must have done something."

"He's been handled," Diana told them. "Zumius. We destroyed the vials he was using to harness special powers from the kids he'd taken—and Lumierna busted his machine. So he has no more powers—which means he can't do much of anything."

"Wait, what?" Viktor's eyes grew wide.

The kids caught them up on everything that had happened. The squad listened with their jaws parted, their shock barely concealed.

"Why, I never!" Phillip said. "So he's done for?"

"Not exactly," Diana said. "He's tied up. We weren't sure what to do with him."

"Say no more!" Viktor saluted Diana. "We're on the job!"

"Thank you," Diana said with relief. "And now—"

Just as she was about to ask them to summon the gods to help the kids return home, the squad sped off. Diana sighed. She knew that she and Imani and the other kids would go home soon enough. The god squad would come back to help them, but she wanted to leave *now.* She wanted to see for herself that everyone back home was okay.

Lightning crackled in the distance. The home rumbled gently beneath their feet before a white burst of light appeared in the room. Diana blinked. It was Zeus. He wore a white tunic and a gold crown and held an enormous staff in his hands.

"You came!" Diana felt like she could melt with relief. "You're here!"

"I have you to thank for it, Diana," he said. "Or rather"—he looked at the other children—"I have *all* of you to thank. Because of your heroism and bravery, my powers have been fully restored, as have the powers of all the gods."

"Zeus?" Imani said slowly. "My father, right?"

"You remember me?" Zeus said.

"I remember everything," she said.

"Ah." He looked at the floor. "There is much we

need to discuss, then. But first things first, are all of you okay?"

"*Now* we are," Aiko replied.

"Zumius is still locked up in the tower," Diana said. "The god squad was heading there a few moments ago."

"Good," Zeus said, and nodded. "We will be transporting Zumius over to Mount Olympus to await his punishment. He wished to harm the gods, so he shall face his punishment in the world of the gods."

Diana exhaled. The gods were once again powerful. And Zumius would pay for what he had done. She thought of her journey this past week. All the obstacles she'd overcome. The numerous times she had felt like all hope was lost, but justice *had* prevailed. *They* had prevailed.

"His hubris led to his downfall," Zeus said. "He presumed children would help him harness potent powers."

And he was wrong. Diana smiled. When all was said and done, kids were the ones to take him down.

"Never underestimate kids," Diana said.

"Indeed, Diana," he replied. "Least of all you."

"Not to be rude, but we have about one hour before my mom comes back," Imani said, glancing at the clock. "I'm planning to tell her everything that went down. She *has* to know. But it might be easier if everyone is safely back home as soon as possible. This is going to be a lot to take in as it is."

"I'd love to go home!" Aristaeus rose from the sofa.

"And so you shall. Thank you again, Aristaeus." Zeus smiled. "And may you never doubt the power of your gifts ever again."

Zeus lit his staff and pointed it at Aristaeus. Aristaeus raised a hand in farewell. A bright light filled the room, vibrating the floor beneath them. Ari was gone.

Aiko was next. Then Lumierna. Before Zeus flashed his torch, they promised to stay in touch. At last, Sakina, Diana, and Augustus remained.

Imani sank into the couch across from them. Zeus turned and smiled at her sympathetically.

"All of this must be very distressing," he said. "To have to relive everything. I'm so sorry. We can talk this out once it's the two of us. I'd love to answer any questions you have. And worry not, I have a concoction." He waved a hand and from thin air appeared a teacup and saucer, which hovered in front of Imani. "It'll need to simmer a bit. Shouldn't be more than a few minutes, and it will make all your concerns go away."

"A tea?" Imani frowned. "For what?"

"To forget." Zeus nodded to the floating tea set. "Once you drink it, it will erase your memories."

"Zeus," Diana began. "Erasing her memories? Her powers? Again?"

"It didn't work the first time," Imani said. "I'm not sure I *want* it to work."

"Don't worry. You have time to say your goodbyes," Zeus assured her. He set the tea on the side table by the sofa. "But this is more powerful than what I tried earlier. A forgetting tea will erase this not only from your conscious memory but from your psyche, without a trace. And as for your power, I can't erase it completely, but I can apply a stronger bond to keep it locked away and hidden."

Imani looked at the tea on the side table, then at Diana, Sakina, and Augustus.

"I don't want to," Imani said finally. "I don't want to drink it. I don't want to forget my memories."

"I can understand your hesitation given what happened," Zeus said slowly. "Your memories coming back to the surface must have been frightful. My powers had been affected and . . ."

"My memories returning—my powers coming to life—were critical in saving us," Imani said.

"Imani's right," Diana said, and nodded. "We were almost caught before we'd even begun."

"I don't want to lose my abilities," Imani said. "I don't want to forget who I am."

"Does this mean you wish to revisit the option I had mentioned back on Themyscira? For you to live with me on Mount Olympus? Your mother will be home soon, and it's certainly a conversation all of us can have."

"No way," Imani interrupted, shaking her head. "Leaving my mother is not going to happen."

"I'm afraid I don't understand," he said. "You wish

to stay *as you are* in the mortal world? Surely you remember how difficult it was, don't you?"

"I know it's complicated to be here, in my world, with the skill I have," Imani said. "It always has been, but even if no one understands me, at least I finally understand myself. Wondering what other people think about me isn't a reason to forget who I am and to *lose* part of what makes me *me.* I am a demigod. I am a descendant of the gods. And"—she smiled at Diana—"I don't want to forget any of this."

Zeus grew silent.

"You are far braver than I realized, Imani," he finally said, resting a hand on her shoulder. "When your mother returns, I think the three of us need to have a conversation."

"I'd love some help in breaking all of this to her," Imani said.

Zeus turned to Augustus and Sakina and Diana. "Who would like to be next?"

Diana's eyes filled with tears. She was relieved her friends were safe, but now they were leaving.

"We save the world and say goodbye. Again," Sakina said sadly.

"I agree. We really gotta stop meeting like this," Augustus said.

"We'll meet again," Diana said. "I promise. Maybe a reunion."

"She promised!" Sakina grinned. "Diana never breaks a promise."

"That's right," Diana told Sakina. "And hey, we're not waiting until the next Charà festival to see each other again. After all I've been through, I think a trip on a Sky Kanga is more than earned!"

"I'm going to hold you to it." Sakina laughed.

Zeus raised his torch, and one by one he tapped Sakina and Augustus. Both of them lit up before vanishing.

Now it was Diana's turn.

"You think *we'll* ever meet again?" Imani asked.

"I hope so," Diana said. "A group like this has got to team up again. Let's hope it's not to fight a monster trying to take over the world."

"Well, whoever dares try had better quake in their boots." Imani winked.

"Ready?" Zeus asked. "Artemis awaits you on the other side to ferry you home."

"Ready as I'll ever be," Diana said. She closed her eyes and felt the torch land gently upon her head. Warmth filled her body. The world blurred around her, but instead of entering a darkened tunnel or terrifying endless dark, she was surrounded by starlight. And instead of fear, Diana felt peace. She smiled. She was going home.

Chapter Thirty-Two

Blue sky appeared above. Clouds floated past. Diana fluttered like a leaf straight into a golden chariot.

"Welcome, dear Diana." It was Artemis. She beamed at Diana. "So wonderful to see you again."

"I made it," Diana said. "I'm really back."

A gentle breeze swept against her face as she glanced around. She pressed her hands against the edge of the chariot. A wave of exhaustion passed through her. She'd been through so much. A brush with a demon, a journey to the Underworld to fight Hades himself, and she had just traveled to the mortal world and taken down the evilest danger of all—Zumius. Now he would be tried for his crimes. Justice would be served.

Diana felt her shoulders relax. It was over. It was really over.

Artemis tugged at the reins. "We are so grateful for your bravery, Diana. You singlehandedly did what so many of us could not do. Let this be a lesson to us gods and goddesses about all that children can do."

"Thank you." Diana smiled.

"Now," Artemis said, "let's get you home."

Diana craned her neck and looked out at the open sea as the stags flew quickly, until at last she saw the cliffsides and the coliseum. She felt light with joy. There it was: Themyscira, her home. Her ordinary—and until quite recently, utterly uneventful—home. After a lifetime of wishing she could leave her island for adventures, what she wanted more than anything now was to be with her mother, Binti, and the women of Themyscira.

Growing closer, Diana saw the remnants of the battle that had pummeled their land. But alongside the damage were new rose hedges, freshly planted around the palace. The pockmarks in the sand had been filled in and covered up. The coliseum was still battered, but they'd fix it—brick by brick they'd put it back into place.

As the chariot lowered, a flicker of worry passed through Diana. Whatever the reasons might have been, she'd left without a word of warning. How mad would Hippolyta be?

All qualms vanished when she saw her mother, Cylinda and Yen, and the other women running up the hill toward her.

"Diana!" her mother said tearfully. In an instant she was engulfed in hugs and kisses. The people she loved so dearly. *Her* people. She was home. Diana felt weak with relief.

"I thought you'd be furious with me," Diana said. "I'm sorry for how I left. It happened so quickly."

"I'm too relieved to be angry," her mother said. "But for heaven's sake . . . the *mortal* world."

"You *are* okay, aren't you?" Aunt Antiope said. She lifted Diana's arms and examined her face.

"I'm okay," she promised. "I'm sorry I worried you."

"You had good reason for what you did."

"I did," Diana said, relieved.

"Diana is being far too modest," Artemis said. "Zeus filled me in on everything. She saved the world. Quite literally."

"I don't know about that," Diana said.

"Yes, the world," Artemis said. "You, Diana, stopped Zumius. You restored the powers of the gods. Thanks to you the world is safe and secure once more."

Diana scrunched her nose, but Artemis *was* right, she realized. This was exactly what she had helped to do.

"She also caused a bit of a stir in the mortal world," Artemis said, winking at Diana. "Apparently, she saved a little girl from quite a tumble. Someone captured the moment on a device, and it made quite the rounds."

"Oh." Diana blushed. "She was falling so fast and the playset was fairly high. I thought she'd get injured."

"Not to worry, Zeus has by now sent a flash across the mortal world. It will wipe everything clean, including the memories of all mortals. But for a good few hours you were quite famous, Diana."

Diana thought about the speed with which she'd run. She'd never fully appreciated this until she'd seen it played back for her. She thought of the slippery building she'd climbed. And when she'd slipped . . .

"There is something I wanted to talk to you about," Diana said. "Something happened in the mortal world. I *did* run fast to save the girl. Faster than I think is truly possible. And . . . other things also happened. Things I didn't think I could do."

"Like what?" her mother asked carefully.

"Well, I've been quite strong at times," Diana said. "I broke out of metal cuffs on the island of Sáz. I lifted a grandfather clock three times my height and broke a window in the Underworld. But each time I always attributed it to how stressed I was and my emotions and adrenaline helping me do things that would otherwise be impossible. But then Zumius told me I could fly. At first, I thought he was out of his mind. Except when I almost fell. No, I *did* fall—from a ledge atop an enormous building when a burst of wind swept through, and I swam with my arms and grabbed on to the building, but I should've fallen straight to the ground. Imani saw it happen, too. I flew, Mother. For the briefest of moments, I did. And later, once I was connected to the machine, *Zumius* flew."

She waited for her mother to laugh. To offer up an explanation Diana hadn't considered before. She waited for Aunt Antiope to offer a pithy remark. Instead, her mother's eyes grew moist.

"Wait," Diana said with a start. "Mother, am I . . . ?"

"I always told you that you were special. I meant it. Yes. There are things you can do. Things that make you incredibly special and that you'll be able to do more once you grow into who you are meant to be. But what you did today? This entire week? Selflessly going headfirst into danger to protect those who need you? *That's* who you are, Diana. Your love for others and your sense of justice will make you one of the greatest to have ever lived."

"Love," Diana repeated. "He said one of my powers was love. When I thought about all of you here on Themyscira and all that would be lost if he won, his machine began to smoke and malfunction."

"Sounds about right," her mother said. "Love is the most powerful force in the world. With all his evil, he could not begin to understand love or how to wield it."

"I'm not sure I understand," Diana admitted.

"There will be plenty of time to get into all of it later," Aunt Antiope said. "I promise. But first we need to celebrate." She smiled. "And we thought for such a great occasion, a gift was in order."

"For me?"

Aunt Antiope leaned down, and only now did Diana see that there had been a sheathed weapon wrapped in leather lying on the grass by her feet. She lifted it now. Unsheathing it, she held it up for Diana to see.

"Wait. It can't be," Diana gasped. "A butterfly sword?"

"The one and only," her mother said. "You said it was your favorite one. I think I heard something about that earlier this week, right?"

"Yes. You told me to put it back on the table," Diana said, and laughed.

"I'm strong enough to admit when I am wrong," said Queen Hippolyta. She smiled. "I think you've proven beyond a shadow of a doubt that you are more than capable of holding this weapon and more."

"The sword is yours," Aunt Antiope said. "I trust you'll handle it well."

Diana held the butterfly sword in her hand. It was sleek and light and perfect. She loved having another weapon in her collection—and a butterfly sword no less! But glancing down at her emerald-encrusted sword, she smiled. This little sword had saved her countless times. She'd dismissed it before, but she realized now that this weapon had been there for her; it was ordinary, yes, and indescribably special.

The women urged Diana toward home. Thelma promised a feast fit for queens. Binti joined the celebration, nuzzling Diana's leg as they headed toward the palace.

Diana couldn't wait to talk more with her mother

about who she was. What her skills were and where they came from. There was so much she didn't know. But there was so much she finally *did* know: she was capable of destroying a demon, exposing Hades, taking down Zumius. And she had saved the world.

Diana glanced back at the horizon, her new sword at her side, with her trusty weapon nestled right along with it. The future remained a question mark. What else might come her way? What other dangers could arise? There was no telling, but right then Diana felt bright and filled with hope. Whatever came, Diana now knew she was meant to help and heal the world—and now she knew she would be ready.

Acknowledgments

A book is never made in a vacuum, and this series is no exception. I am humbled and honored to have been part of Diana's iconic world. Thank you so much to my fearless editor, Sasha Henriques, for your insights and collaboration. It was a gift to work with you. Thank you to Chelsea Eberly for inviting me to write this series. Thank you to the entire team at Random House and Warner Bros., including Michelle Nagler, Janet Foley, Barbara Bakowski, Kris Kam, Tara Grieco, and Ben Harper. Thank you to Alessia Trunfio for the beautiful covers throughout this series. Thank you also to Cylinda Parga, Yen M. Tang, Ayesha Mattu, Tracy Lopez, Becky Albertalli, S. K. Ali, Sabaa Tahir, and Samira Ahmed for your support and friendship. And endless gratitude to my husband and my boys. Because of you, I know that love is truly the greatest superpower there is. And last, but certainly not least, thank *you,* dear reader. Thank you for reading this story and for welcoming this series into your homes, your classrooms, and your libraries. Your support means the world.

About the Author

Aisha Saeed is the *New York Times* bestselling author of *Amal Unbound.* She is a Pakistani American writer, teacher, and attorney who is also the author of *Written in the Stars, Aladdin: Far from Agrabah,* and *Bilal Cooks Daal,* as well as the other books in the Wonder Woman Adventures series. She has been featured on MTV, *HuffPost,* NBC, and the BBC, and her writing has appeared in publications including the *ALAN Review* and the *Orlando Sentinel.* As a founding member of the nonprofit We Need Diverse Books, she is helping change the conversation about inclusive representation in books. Aisha lives in Atlanta with her husband and sons.

aishasaeed.com